SHOWDOWN AT TOPEZ

All Brett Calhoun wanted to do was to build his railway from the quiet town of Topez to San Caldiz on the Rio Grande. But when a gang of bandits, led by the redoubtable Alphonso, takes over the town, Brett is unwillingly dragged into the fight to restore it to its rightful rulers. To make matters worse, a marauding band of Apaches also takes a keen interest in the proceedings, and Brett's personal life is complicated by the beautiful Carmen. Peace would be a long time coming to Topez.

Books by Tom Parry
in the Linford Western Library:

THE BANDIT TRAIL
LAST STAGE TO SULA
RICCO, SON OF RINGO

TOM PARRY

SHOWDOWN AT TOPEZ

Complete and Unabridged

LINFORD
Leicester

First published in Great Britain in 2002 by
Robert Hale Limited
London

First Linford Edition
published 2003
by arrangement with
Robert Hale Limited
London

British Library CIP Data

Parry, Tom
  Showdown at Topez.—Large print ed.—
  Linford western library
  1. Western stories
  2. Large type books
  I. Title
  823.9′14 [F]

ISBN 1–8439–5059–6

Published by
F. A. Thorpe (Publishing)
Anstey, Leicestershire

Set by Words & Graphics Ltd.
Anstey, Leicestershire
Printed and bound in Great Britain by
T. J. International Ltd., Padstow, Cornwall

This book is printed on acid-free paper

1

About thirty armed men rode into Topez. The precise number was immaterial since it was not their exact composition which was important but their objective. Namely to take over the town.

The townsfolk who became aware of the new arrivals at first regarded them with a mixture of suspicion and hope. Maybe, after all, they were on their way to some other town. The fact that they had all assembled in the town's square didn't have any significance, did it? Other riders who came into the town would head for the square. In the middle there was the town pump from which they could quench their thirst. There were also four troughs, one on each corner of the square, from which their horses could drink. Then some riders would toss a coin to old Pablo who had operated the pump for them. Some would even cross themselves when they passed the statue of the Virgin Mary outside the church. Then they would ride on their way.

These men, however, didn't show any intention of riding away. The townsfolk watched as half a dozen of them dismounted and went towards the army barracks. The sentry on duty had been watching them with growing unease. Now, as they walked purposefully towards him the unease changed to fear. He knew that it was his duty to stand his ground but all his instincts told him to ignore duty and dive inside the gate.

In a space of a few seconds it had become too late for him to beat a retreat. The leader of the half-dozen men was now standing in front of him. He was a tall man with a pock-marked face and a thin moustache. 'Take me to see your lieutenant,' he commanded.

The guard breathed a silent sigh of relief. Maybe things weren't going to be too bad after all. The man in front of him had asked politely to see the lieutenant. All he had to do was to take him inside to see Lieutenant Calvero and everything would then return to normal. After all, although these men were carrying guns their weapons were still in their holsters.

'I can only take one of you through to see the lieutenant,' he pointed out.

'That's all right. My men can wait here.'

The guard breathed another sigh of relief as he unbolted the door. The two men stepped inside the side gate and the guard locked it after them.

The parade ground was empty as the two crossed it in silence. Although the guard had relaxed after his initial fright there was still a lingering unease in his mind. Why should a large number of men ride into the town? He had seen their guns and they had all been cleaned and were shining the same as the soldiers in the barracks ahead. These men were either in the army, or, more than likely, they were deserters who had once been in the army. Still, it was none of his business. The lieutenant could sort it out. After all, that's what he was getting paid for.

They came to a large door. The guard knocked. A voice from the other side asked who was there. The guard identified himself and the door was opened. 'Here's somebody to see the lieutenant,' he stated.

'All right, I'll take him inside.'

The guard was relieved that his responsibility had come to an end. He walked back to his position by the gate in a happier frame of mind than when he had crossed the parade ground five minutes before. He could even relax and think what was ahead of him when he had finished his spell of duty. He would be relieved by another guard and he would go home to his lovely wife, Carmen. She would have made him a tasty meal of soup and tortillas — Carmen made the best tortillas in Topez. Then afterwards they would go to bed and make love. Carmen, like many Mexican women, had a passionate nature. As he reached the gate there was a slight smile on his face as his thoughts dwelt on Carmen.

It was at that moment that the silence was broken by the sound of several shots from inside the barracks. The guard reached for his revolver. Too late he realized that there were already guns in the hands of the men outside the gate. He instinctively knew that he would never be returning to his beloved Carmen as their bullets thudded into him.

2

In the mountains the mayor, his cronies and most of the army garrison had had a good hunt. The chief result of their excursion into the mountains — a magnificent wild boar — lay dead at their feet. In addition there was a satisfactory pile of rabbits which had been shot by the army marksmen. These would be distributed among the poorer families of Topez. The boar would be roasted the following day in the centre of the town square.

'We'll have a fiesta,' said the mayor, Luis Montez, rubbing his hands. He was a typical short, squat Mexican. Even riding his horse in the mountains he obstinately wore his chain of office. The other distinguishing feature was his moustache which he had managed to cultivate so that it was bigger and curlier than those of most of his contemporaries.

The others in the hunting party signified their agreement. 'It'll cost us a large sum of money,' said the town clerk, a thin man named Ballisto.

'We've got money in the town coffers,' said Luis, dismissively. 'Anyhow we haven't had a fiesta this year. The townsfolk deserve a fiesta. They're hard working and law abiding.'

'And the mayor will get the praise for the fiesta,' whispered one of the soldiers to his companion.

'We'd better start moving,' said Luis.

A sergeant organized a few of the soldiers to tie the boar to some poles and carry it between them while some of the other soldiers took charge of their horses and led them down the mountain towards Topez. The general opinion was that it had been a successful day. In the past they had often spent a day hunting in the mountains with hardly anything to show for it in the end. Now there was the prospect of a fiesta which would be held in a few day's time. The fiesta meant music, dancing, drinking and at the end of it making love — and not necessarily to your own wife.

'I suppose you'll be bringing your wife,' said one of the soldiers, named Lamas.

'Of course I will,' his companion, Sebastian, replied, 'Why?'

'Oh, nothing. Except that I've heard that she's one of the best dancers in Topez.'

'She *is* the best dancer,' replied the other, indignantly. 'Just you wait and see.'

Actually Lamas fancied Sebastian's wife. She was a beautiful half-caste named Alicia. He couldn't imagine how such a beautiful creature could have married such a worm as Sebastian. Anyhow, if everything went according to plan at the fiesta, after the wine had began flowing freely, he, Lamas, had already hatched a plan to seduce the beautiful Alicia. He knew that Sebastian could not hold his liquor. After half a dozen stoups of wine Lamas would be out for the count. That was when he, Lamas, would be able to make his move. He already knew that Alicia hadn't flinched under his admiring glances. He was generally regarded as the most handsome private in the army and he had a reputation as a women's man. His own wife, Rosita, was due to have another baby in a few weeks' time and she was now so shapeless that he had no desire to make love to her. However, the fiesta would be an ideal opportunity for him to fulfil his sexual appetites. His mouth watered at the thought.

At that moment a soldier appeared over the brow of the hill. He was obviously in a distressed state. He half stumbled, half ran, towards the hunting party.

'What is it?' demanded the sergeant, when the soldier reached him.

'Lieutenant Calvero has been shot,' he gasped. 'About thirty bandits have taken over the town.'

Consternation spread like wildfire among the hunting party. It was mirrored in the faces of the soldiers, the mayor and his followers.

'What do you mean, taken over the town?' asked the mayor, with trepidation.

'They've gathered the townsfolk in the church. Their leader made a speech. He told them that nothing would be changed, except that he would now be the mayor and he and his men would be running the town.'

'What about the soldiers in the barracks?' demanded the sergeant.

'Never mind the soldiers,' said Luis, angrily. 'What about my town?'

'There were only a dozen or so left,' the bearer of ill tidings reminded them. 'They have all been rounded up. They are now in the cells. The leader, his name is Alphonso, by the way, said he would shoot them all if any of the rest of you decide to attack the town.'

'We can't let them get away with this,' stormed Luis. 'We must attack them.'

'That isn't all,' said the messenger. 'Alphonso sent me here and said I was to make sure that I delivered the rest of the message.'

'All right, what is it?' demanded Luis, impatiently.

'Alphonso said that he will start killing the townsfolk one by one if you and the soldiers ever come near the town again.'

3

In Topez everything was relatively calm for a town which had just surrendered its freedom to a gang of bandits. Alphonso had taken up his position in the mayor's office. The guard at the gate of the barracks had been replaced by one of his men. Several of his other men were marching conspicuously in the square. They held their rifles at the ready and their faces showed that at the slightest provocation they were prepared to use them. True, none of the usual traders had set up their stalls in the square, but Alphonso was confident that even that would return to normal the following day. In the meantime the only other difference was that the church bell was ringing at a time when it would normally be silent.

People put their heads out through their doorways. What could it mean, the church bell ringing at this time in the evening? The question was bounced back and forth like a tennis ball until one of the bandits enlightened them with the answer. They were all to attend church straightaway. The priest had an announcement to make.

The priest? Father Mondello? What could he possibly have to say to them at this hour of the day? Unless it was something about the bandits. Yes, that was it, he was going to tell them to resist the bandits. He was going to pray for them and give them the spiritual strength to fight the bandits. Those who had up to now been drifting slowly out of their houses began to head towards the church with a new purpose in their steps.

The church was soon packed. Since it was physically impossible for the whole population of Topez to fit inside it, dozens of others were crammed near the open door where they would be able to catch Father Mondello's voice. After all he was a powerful speaker

— particularly when he was preaching against the hateful Romans. They waited eagerly for his first announcement.

Those inside the church were the first to realize that it was not Father Mondello but the bandit, Alphonso, who would be making an announcement. They were shocked to see him take his place in the pulpit exactly as though he were a priest. A gasp of horror went round the congregation at the nerve of the bandit. Surely he would be condemned to hell-fire for eternity for such an act of desecration!

'I'm not going to take up much of your time,' began Alphonso. 'I'm just going to let you know what most of you already know — my men and I have taken over the town. I will be the new mayor. Everything will carry on as before. The market stalls will open tomorrow as usual. If any stall is not open then the person whose stall it is will be shot.'

A gasp of horror ran through the

congregation, not so much at the words themselves but at the casual manner in which they were delivered. If anyone had any doubts beforehand that Alphonso was now their master these had now been immediately dispelled. His next words emphasized the point.

'Nobody will leave Topez unless I give them permission. If anybody tries to sneak out and he is successful in evading my guards I will throw all the members of their family into jail. Then I will take them out one by one every morning and shoot them until there are none left. Do I make myself clear?'

The audience realized that Alphonso had closed the door on there being any attempts to escape to San Caldiz, which was the nearest large town, about twenty miles away.

'Are there any questions?'

'Yes, I've got one.' A tall man who obviously wasn't a Mexican stood up in the back of the church. 'I'm not a Mexican. I'm an American citizen. You've got no right to keep me prisoner here in this town.'

'I'm afraid that you have no choice, *señor*. What is your name?'

'Calhoun. Brett Calhoun.'

'Well, Mr Calhoun, I'm afraid you must stay here. This town in now under military law. If you do nothing to break the law you can stay in the town and carry on with whatever you were doing yesterday. Which is — '

'I was in charge of building a railway to San Caldiz.'

'A very worthwhile task. When I rode in I saw that the railway only ran for a few miles out of the town.'

'That's right. I'd say that we've only completed about a quarter of it.'

'As I said, it's a worthwhile task and one which I hope you will continue with.'

'I don't seem to have much choice, do I?' said Brett, bitterly.

'No, *señor*, you haven't,' said Alphonso, emphatically. 'And now to show that I want this town to thrive and prosper I have one suggestion.' The audience waited while he inserted a dramatic pause. 'Tonight the cantinas will serve free wine. Tonight will be a celebration of the first night of a new regime. It will be a regime that will bring peace and harmony as long as my orders are obeyed.'

The thought of free wine at the six cantinas in the town had already made many of the men stand up and head for the exit. Some of their wives tried vainly to restrain them. Brett watched as the men pushed and jostled in their efforts to be the first to get to their cantina. He knew that he was witnessing the end of an era for the town. He had spent six months here building his railway and he had enjoyed the relaxed atmosphere, even though it meant that many of his workers were often too relaxed, and he would have to bully them in getting on with their work. However they would start work again with a smile. Yes, that was it, it was a happy town. People smiled when they greeted you in the street. It had no class distinctions, since everybody worked for a living, nearly all of them with their hands. But it didn't take a genius to work out that everything was now going to change. A dictator had taken over. He'd learned enough from his history books to know that dictators inevitably brought death and misery.

He was so wrapped up in his thoughts that he hadn't noticed that almost all the congregation had left the church. Alphonso, too, had left the pulpit. Brett glanced at the gold-plated effigy of Christ which stood in front of the west window. He wasn't a religious man, although back home in Texas he used to attend the Methodist church with the rest of his family.

On impulse he closed his eyes. If you've any miracles left, spare one for Topez, he prayed.

4

Luis and his hunting party were seated on the grass around the dead boar. To Chianto, who was one of the more imaginative members of the hunting party, the boar seemed to have a triumphant gleam in its eye. It seemed to be saying, serve you right for killing me, now I've got my revenge.

'Somebody obviously told this Alphonso that we were going hunting,' said Luis, gloomily.

'Obviously,' said his deputy, a tall man for a Mexican, named Graciano. He had a squint which, together with his thin moustache, gave him a sinister appearance.

'Lieutenant Calvero — dead,' said the distraught sergeant. 'I don't believe it.'

'It's true,' said the soldier who had brought the news. 'And the sentry on the gate. The one with the pretty wife, Carmen.'

'I know her,' said one of the soldiers. 'She used to make lovely tortillas. I've called at her house to have some when her husband, Fernando, was on duty.'

'I bet tortillas wasn't all she gave you,' said one of the other soldiers. There was general laughter.

'All right, that's enough,' snapped Luis, who felt that he should re-establish his authority. 'The question is, what are we going to do now?'

'We haven't got any choice,' said Chianto. 'We'll have to stay up here in the mountains.'

The majority looked at him with surprise, due to the fact that he had already worked out their next move, while they had barely come to terms with their present position.

'I would have thought that's obvious,' snapped Luis, who was among the majority who hadn't considered their future, but who, under no circumstances, wished to lose face by confessing the fact.

'We'll have to find somewhere to camp,' said Graciano.

'It'll have to be somewhere near where we can get running water,' supplied the sergeant.

'That'll mean going even further away from Topez,' complained Luis.

'We haven't got any choice,' the sergeant pointed out reasonably. 'There aren't any springs or streams around here. We'll have to go nearer San Caldiz. There's a mountain stream there which flows into the Rio Grande. At least we'll always have fresh water.'

'I don't fancy spending weeks — months even — camped up here in the mountains,' grumbled Luis.

'We haven't got any choice,' stated Graciano, positively. 'When we've made our camp we can think of a way of taking Topez from Alphonso and his bandits.'

'Someone can ride to San Caldiz and notify the president that Alphonso and his gang of murderers have taken over

Topez,' suggested Chianto.

Once again the upstart, who considered himself a writer, had come up with a good idea. Luis scowled. It was his prerogative to have ideas. At the earliest opportunity he would get rid of this pain in the arse. Wait a minute! Here was an ideal opportunity.

'I suggest that you ride to San Caldiz to see the President,' said Luis, barely able to conceal his delight at being able to get rid of this thorn in the flesh.

Chianto did not receive the suggestion too happily. The main drawback to Luis's suggestion was that he was not a particularly good horseman. He didn't fancy riding all the way to San Caldiz, but looking at the expectant faces around him, he knew that he had no choice.

'All right,' he said, resignedly. 'I'll be on my way.'

'You'd better take some food with you,' said the sergeant, tossing him a couple of rabbits.

Chianto set off on a trail which

would take him down to the valley and the main route towards San Caldiz. It was quicker to descend the mountain than to climb it and he was soon in sight of the plain. Although he viewed his proposed journey with trepidation, he was happy to be going down to the plain instead of being forced to live up in the mountains. For one thing it was warmer down on the plain. For another he would be escaping from that fool, Luis. He had no faith in Luis's mental powers, which he put on a par with a lizard's. He smiled at the metaphor. He was still smiling when the bullet of one of Alphonso's gunmen hit him in the heart.

5

In the one hotel in Topez, which was incongruously named The Ritz, Brett sat in the small side room which was just as incongruously named the bar. Any similarity to a bar in an American hotel was non-existent. This bar consisted of a couple of well-worn tables and their accompanying chairs. There were no drinks on display. To attract the attention of the barman, a morose character named Jose, one banged on the table. He would then appear from behind a curtain with a bottle of tequila and refill your glass. Normally Brett was not a great advocate of drinking tequila. But tonight was different. A few hours ago his well-ordered existence in Topez had been shattered by the arrival of Alphonso and his gangsters. Tonight he felt like drowning his sorrows.

Brett banged on the table and Jose

appeared as promptly as a jack-in-the-box.

'What do you think is going to happen now?' demanded Brett, as Jose refilled his glass.

'We just have to wait,' said Jose, with an expressive shrug.

'Wait for what?' demanded a puzzled Brett.

'Until they go away,' stated Jose. His tone indicated that he would have thought that was obvious — even to an American.

'Won't somebody be going to San Caldiz to notify the President?' demanded Brett.

'Who's going to go? Who's going to risk their lives? Not only their own lives but the lives of their family they have left behind?'

'You've got a point there,' said Brett, studying his glass, as though expecting to find a solution inside. Jose showed signs of disappearing. 'You might as well leave that bottle,' said Brett, peeling off an American dollar bill from a roll. 'It will save you popping in and out.'

Alphonso had said that things must go on as before, but how could they? He had cut the telegraph wires which connected the town to San Caldiz. That meant that when it came time for him to order fresh supplies to construct the railway he would not be able to do so. He had enough rail and sleepers in the stores to last him, say, a couple of weeks, but what would happen after that? That was just one of the problems. What about paying the men? The bank manager would not be able to get in touch with his head office to arrange credit, so he would not be able to pay his three dozen or so workers. Wait a minute! There was something there that Alphonso hadn't considered. The authorities in San Caldiz would realize that the telegraph lines were down. They would automatically send out a few engineers to investigate the fact. They would discover that the wires had been deliberately cut and report the

26

fact back to the head office. The authorities would be alerted that something unusual was going on in Topez. The army would be alerted. And soon that would be the end of Alphonso.

He was delighted that he had spotted the flaw in Alphonso's plan. In fact he was so delighted that he drained his glass of tequila. He poured another. He was vaguely aware that he was getting drunk. It was not an unpleasant feeling. He owed it to himself to have a celebration; after all, he had just calculated how Alphonso's plan would fail. He was vaguely aware that there seemed to be a considerable amount of noise outside. Of course, he remembered now. Alphonso had decreed that the cantinas should serve free drinks. And it sounded as though many of the good people of Topez were taking advantage of the offer.

Normally Brett, after emptying the bottle of tequila, would have gone upstairs to his narrow bedroom. But curiosity impelled him to go outside the hotel and view the noisy activities there. He was surprised to see that there was dancing in the square. A group of musicians had appeared on a makeshift stage in the centre and several couples were dancing around them. Well, some were dancing, while others were lurching around with their wives in their arms. Brett surveyed them benevolently. He recognized some of the men as belonging to his labour force. Well, let them enjoy themselves tonight courtesy of the free drinks supplied by Alphonso.

He strolled round the square enjoying the cool night air. He came to an alleyway where he saw two vague figures who at first sight appeared to be in a close embrace. He was about to pass when the woman gave a loud scream. It was unnoticed in the general noise of the musicians and the shrieks of excitement of the dancers. Brett hesitated. It was none of his business. Maybe they were a husband and wife engaged in one of their routine daily arguments. Or maybe a husband and somebody else's wife engaged in a little extra-marital activity.

He turned away and was about to continue with his stroll when the woman gave another piercing scream — this time even louder than the one before. Brett turned and stared into the dark alleyway. The two figures were still indistinct but he could make out that they were still struggling. Brett hesitated. It really wasn't any of his business.

Suddenly he saw the gleam of a knife. His reaction was automatic. He dived into the alleyway. The figures were only a few metres inside. The man drew away from the woman at Brett's approach. Brett could see the knife clearly now. It was raised and its owner had now changed the direction of its aim. It was about to descend towards him. He instinctively stepped close to the man and seized his arm. He twisted it until he heard the satisfying 'clunk' which told him that the knife had fallen out of the man's grasp and landed on the ground. There was a choked scream, but this time it came from the man and not from the woman. Brett continued twisting the man's arm. His body was pressed against him so that he could not slide out of Brett's grasp. The man hurled a string of swear words at him. Brett continued to force his arm upwards. The man had given up struggling and was now standing on his toes to try to alleviate the excruciating pain. Suddenly the scream the man had uttered a few moments ago was nothing compared to the one which now rent the air. It was caused by Brett pulling the man's collar bone out of its socket.

'I don't think you'll be pulling a knife on anyone for quite a while,' said Brett, as he gasped for breath.

His satisfaction was short-lived. There was the 'click' of a revolver being levelled behind him.

6

Luis and his men had camped for the night. They had arrived at their destination, having ridden steadily to reach it before sunset. There was an air of despondency about the hunting party.

'I wonder how long we'll have to stay up here?' asked Graciano.

'We'll stay here until we decide what our next move will be,' stated Luis.

'We've still got our guns,' said the sergeant. 'Maybe we can attack Topez and take the bandits by surprise.'

'They'll kill our wives and children if we try to do that,' stated Graciano.

'They can have my wife,' said one of the soldiers. 'I've been trying to get rid of her for ages.' The laughter which greeted his remark was muted, showing how low was the general mood of the camp.

'All right,' said Luis. 'We'll all turn in. We'll decide what we're going to do next in the morning.'

'At least we won't be short of food for a couple of days,' said Graciano, indicating the boar which they had brought with them.

The hunting party had assumed that they were the only occupants of that particular stretch of mountainside. They would have been considerably surprised to learn that their arrival had been closely monitored — not by Mexicans, but by a hunting party of Indians. They were Apaches who had been forced over the border because they themselves had been hunted in America by the authorities who did not see eye to eye with their practice of descending on unsuspecting settlers, killing them and stealing their livestock. And finally scalping them. The Apaches had been puzzled by the arrival of the Mexicans and were now discussing the situation.

'Let's attack them,' said a hot-headed

brave named Blue Lightning.

'We've got to find out what they're doing here first,' said the chief, an old man named White Beard who had survived several battles with the pale-faces.

'Their wild boar looks very tasty,' said a rather plump member of the raiding party.

'Why don't we go down and steal it when they are sleeping?' demanded his friend, who was as thin as the other was fat.

'Yes, that might be possible,' said White Beard, thoughtfully. He had noticed that the wild boar had been deposited some distance from the camp. He had also noticed that the Mexicans had not bothered to arrange to mount a guard for the night.

The Apaches waited. They were good at waiting. Finally, when they were convinced that the last soldiers were asleep, they crept forward silently. They were good too, at creeping forward silently.

Blue Lightning led the way. He headed for the boar which the Mexicans had deposited in a slight hollow. He had almost reached it when a soldier stepped from behind a tree where he had been relieving himself. In the moonlight the Apache was clearly visible. The soldier opened his mouth to yell a warning, but before the words came out a tell-tale gash of blood spurted from his neck where Blue Lightning had drawn his hunting knife across it with startling rapidity. The intended shout ended up as a death gurgle and the soldier sank to the ground.

Blue Lightning now stood stock still, having signalled to his accompanying braves to do the same. They waited for several minutes before he signalled to them again. This time he pointed to the boar. His message was clear — carry the animal away from the camp.

Two of the braves picked the boar up and began slowly to ascend the mountain. When they reached their camp White Beard examined the boar critically.

'It looks as though it has been killed within the last twenty-four hours,' he announced. The Apaches were good at telling how long a creature or man had been killed since they were experts in that field themselves.

7

Brett was standing in front of Alphonso's desk in the Mayor's office. He had been brought there at gunpoint by the soldier who had come up behind him after his fight in the alley.

'I could have you shot for breaking one of my soldier's arms,' said Alphonso, coldly.

'I didn't know he was a soldier,' Brett pointed out reasonably. 'It was dark.'

'I could use you as an example,' continued Alphonso, as if Brett hadn't spoken. 'There are several Americans staying in Topez. They probably think they are exempt from the martial law which I have decreed.' By the light of the lamp which hung from the ceiling the pock marks on his face appeared to be deeper.

'I've told you I didn't know he was one of your soldiers,' said Brett, irritably.

'Anyhow he shouldn't have been attacking the woman. You should keep better control over your men.'

Even by the half light of the lamp Brett could see the anger on Alphonso's face.

'I'm in charge here, and I'll do what I like,' he stormed, thumping his desk for emphasis.

Brett wisely held his tongue. Alphonso studied him. 'You must be quite strong to break a man's arm,' he observed, more calmly.

'I don't believe in sitting in my office and letting my men do all the work,' said Brett, drily. 'I help out with laying the rails from time to time.'

'Ah, yes, of course, the railway,' said Alphonso, thoughtfully. The bandit seemed to have left his anger behind, Brett observed thankfully. 'How many days' supply have you in the store to carry on working?'

Brett had about three weeks' supply but there was no way that Alphonso would know that. 'About a week,' he lied.

Alphonso studied his face as if deciding whether he was lying or not. Finally he said, 'You can consider yourself lucky, *gringo*. If I didn't need you to keep on building the railway you would be shot in the morning.'

Inwardly Brett breathed a sigh of relief although he kept his face impassive. 'I can go now then?'

'I don't see why you should get away scot free,' snapped Alphonso. 'You'll spend a night in the cells.'

He signalled to the guard who had been standing by the door. Brett shrugged. He turned and followed the guard out of the office and along several corridors before coming to a corridor which held strong steel doors, obviously intended to keep evil-doers inside. Although in his case, decided Brett, he was a man more sinned against than sinning.

★ ★ ★

Brett was awakened by the pale light of dawn filtering through the bars of the window of his cell. He stretched and yawned. He was surprised that he had slept so soundly. After a few minutes there was the sound of activity in the corridor outside. Time to go home, thought Brett, hopefully.

The key was inserted in the lock. A uniformed guard opened the door. To Brett's surprise he ushered in a woman. His surprise increased when he realized she was carrying a dish and from under the cover came the delicious smell of newly cooked tortillas.

'My name is Carmen,' she introduced herself. 'I make the best tortillas in Topez.'

Brett smiled. 'That's the best introduction I've heard. My name is Brett Calhoun.'

'I know. I've seen you around Topez. Now eat while the tortillas are still warm.'

Brett needed no second invitation. While he was eating, Carmen began to speak.

'These are a thank-you gift for saving

me from that bastard of a soldier last night.'

'So you were the other person in the alley,' said Brett, through a mouthful of tortilla.

'That's right. I'd come here to the barracks to make arrangements for my husband's body.'

'I don't understand,' said a puzzled Brett.

'My husband was a soldier. He was the guard on the gate when these scum arrived.' She waved an all-embracing hand to indicate that the scum meant Alphonso and his men. 'I said farewell to him and made arrangements to have his body sent to the undertakers.' She made the statement without apparent emotion although she betrayed her tension in the way she was twisting the cloth she had brought with her into a tight knot.

'I'm sorry,' said Brett, inadequately.

'Well, anyhow, Alphonso ordered a soldier to take me back to my house. The soldier had ideas of his own, as you discovered. I was lucky that you arrived in time. I can't thank you enough.'

'You've more than thanked me enough already by bringing me those delicious tortillas,' said Brett, wiping his lips with the back of his hand.

'Here, let me,' said Carmen. She came close to him and carefully wiped the crumbs from his lips with her cloth. Her nearness stirred something in Brett which he had thought had lain dormant for ages. In fact he had taken the position of building the railway to escape from the memory of a woman. The woman's name had been Ruth and everything had been in place for their wedding. Then suddenly, out of the blue, his brother Patrick had returned from the army. Everything had changed. Within a week Ruth had confessed to him that she was in love with Patrick and that they intended getting married in a week's time.

The blow had been too much for Brett. He spent a week drinking. On the night before the wedding he had turned up at his brother's house. He had been invited in, Patrick thinking that Brett had finally come to his senses and was going to let bygones be bygones. Instead Brett gave his brother the biggest hiding he had ever had in his life. Although Patrick had been in the army and was reasonably fit he was no match for Brett's combination of strength and anger.

Before he left Brett delivered the one final message. 'This is the last time you'll see me,' he told the bleeding figure on the floor. 'I'm going away and I won't be back. By the way, here's my wedding present.' So saying he tossed an envelope containing a thousand dollars on to the floor near his brother.

As a result he had come to Mexico. Now here he was with the beautiful Carmen — and there was no argument that she was beautiful — with her inviting lips almost touching his. He could read the message in her eyes.

Go on, kiss me, it said. You know you want to more than anything in the world.

Suddenly the tension was broken. Brett drew away. 'Thanks again for the tortillas,' he said, hoping it concealed his awkwardness.

Carmen was less successful in hiding her disappointment. Her eyes flashed with scorn. She had offered the gringo her lips, and who knows what more delights later. She knew that most of the single men and half the married ones in Topez would have jumped at the chance she had offered. But not the gringo. Oh, no, she was a Mexican, and therefore she was condemned in his eyes to remain less than an American woman. She felt like spitting. If it had not been that she owed him a considerable debt in that he had fought the soldier for her in the alley she would have put the thought into practice. Instead she scooped up the dish and the cloth, turned on her heel, and flounced out through the door.

Brett's eyes followed her. His mind was still dwelling on his missed opportunity so much that he almost didn't take in the guard's words. 'You can go too,' the guard was saying.

8

In the mountains Luis and his followers were staring in disbelief at the place where the boar had been the night before but which was now an empty piece of mountainside, the boar's previous presence only being discernible by the fact that the grass under it had been flattened slightly.

'It's gone,' said Luis, stating the obvious.

'Perhaps somebody moved it,' suggested Graciano. His gaze took in the soldiers who shook their heads collectively.

'Who could have taken it?' demanded Luis. This brought on more head shaking accompanied by shoulder shrugging at the mayor's stupid question.

'Perhaps the foxes had it,' suggested one of the soldiers.

'Don't be stupid,' said another, 'it

would take a whole team of foxes to move it. And they would leave blood and bones behind.'

Luis arrived at the only other possibility. 'Someone stole it,' he announced. The thirty-or-so-strong party digested the statement individually and collectively.

'It means that yesterday somebody was watching us,' stated the sergeant. Now that the lieutenant had been killed he was next in line for promotion. He was therefore determined to push himself forward at every opportunity.

'I would have thought that's obvious,' said Graciano.

'Bandits,' suggested a soldier.

'That's a possibility,' agreed Luis, thoughtfully. 'There are gangs of bandits up here in the mountains.'

One of the soldiers who had wandered away from the main group suddenly give a startled shout. 'Over here,' he cried.

When the party joined him they found the cause of his distress. The soldier who been killed the night before was lying in some long grass, face upwards, with a gory red necklace emblazoned on his throat.

'It's Paulo,' said one of the soldiers.

'It was Paulo,' corrected the sergeant.

'The bandits must have killed him,' stated Graciano.

'If it *was* bandits,' said the sergeant, secretly pleased to get his own back on that old fool Graciano. He beckoned to an Indian who was the tracker of the party. 'Eagle Eye, see if you can find any tracks of the raiding party last night. While Eagle Eye is searching for them it would be best if everyone stayed where they are to avoid making any more tracks.'

'That makes sense,' growled Luis, who felt that he had been left out of the decision-making.

It wasn't long before Eagle Eye came back with a pronouncement. 'It was Apaches,' he announced.

A collective shiver ran though the party. They knew the deadly reputation of the Apaches. They knew that they were Indians who did most of their killing at night, in contrast to some Indian tribes who believed that the dead man's spirit would stay on earth to haunt them if they killed an enemy at night.

'How do you know they're Apaches?' demanded Luis.

'Because one of them lost this.' Eagle Eye held up a large feather. 'It's an eagle feather worn by an Apache warrior. He must have killed half a dozen pale-faces before he is entitled to wear this with his other feathers.'

'If it was an Apache why didn't he scalp Paulo?' demanded the sergeant.

'Perhaps he wanted us to think it wasn't an Apache who killed Paulo,' suggested a soldier named Rodriguez who was considered to be the cleverest of the privates.

'Yes, that could be the reason,' concurred Luis. 'The question is what are we going to do now?'

'I'm going to get some of my men to bury Paulo,' said the sergeant, 'before the buzzards get to him.

When Paulo was finally buried, with the customary gun salute ignored in order to save ammunition, Luis took charge, having had time to work out what to do next.

'We'll have a meal here from the rabbits we shot yesterday. Then we'll move from here. We don't want to stay here and have our throats cut by the Apaches. We'll have to move further down the mountainside towards the plain. We'll camp there and wait until Chianto returns from San Caldiz with the President's soldiers.'

'What about water?' demanded the sergeant. 'We camped here up in the mountains so that we could have a supply of water. If we go down nearer the plain, there won't be any water.'

Why hadn't he thought of that? Luis asked himself irritably. Aloud he said, 'We'll just have to fill every canteen and container we've got.'

'And pray for rain,' whispered Rodriguez to one of his companions.

9

Brett was sitting impatiently on his horse in the square. He had gone back to the hotel, washed and shaved and was now waiting for the rest of his gang of workmen to appear. He knew that many of them would have sore heads after drinking their fill of free tequila last night. His own head was none too clear. But that had less to do with the wine than his encounter with Carmen an hour or so earlier.

He couldn't rid his mind of the look of scorn she had given him when he had refused the blatant invitation of her lips. Her lips had only been inches away from his and she and he had both stayed in that position for what seemed like an age. Her lips had been slightly parted — he could still see them now. Her face had been so close that even in the dim light of the cell he could sense its perfect beauty. He had seen her of course when she had been out walking with her ex-husband, the lieutenant, but protocol had decreed that he should not stare at her. Even so he had not been able to ignore the impression that she was the most beautiful woman in Topez.

Why hadn't he kissed her? It wasn't as if he was committing himself to a lasting relationship with her. She was offering her lips as a way of saying thank you for saving her from the attentions of the soldier the previous night. It had been as simple as that. She had brought him the tortillas to show her gratitude, but had wished to seal the matter with a kiss. And he had spurned her. He had seen the surprise and then the scorn of her expression as clearly as if it had been caught on one of the new cameras which were now appearing in America.

His men had began to appear. Most of them avoided catching his eye, knowing that they were late for work.

He automatically counted them. There were sixteen at that moment. Another fourteen to come. Perhaps Carmen had concluded he was one of those effeminate men who were to be seen in the theatres. His blood ran cold at the thought.

Another half-dozen of his men materialized. He wondered briefly whether he might as well move off now, rather than wait for the rest. If they wanted to get paid for working today it was up to them. He had wasted enough time as it was.

He was about to ride off when a familiar figure appeared in the square. It was Carmen. Although all the men had eyes for her, it was obvious that she had eyes only for him. Her body swayed temptingly as she moved towards him. To Brett it seemed that her movements had become more sensuous in order to hold his attention. He was still on his horse and was undecided what to do. Should he climb down and greet her, or should he stay on his horse?

He decided on the former course of action. He jumped down from his horse just as she reached him.

'Hullo, Carmen,' he said. He was aware of the inadequacy of the greeting as soon as he uttered the words.

She stared at him as though trying to memorize his face. He knew that he was beginning to get hot under the collar. He knew that all his men were staring at him, too, puzzled about exactly what was going on.

'I've come to thank you for last night.' The puzzlement on the men's faces turned to astonishment and then to shock. Surely the *gringo* hadn't spent the night with the delectable Carmen, and her husband barely cold on the slab?

Brett waited for her to continue. He sensed that she was getting her own back for the humiliation she had suffered in the prison cell.

'You did me a great favour.'

Dimly Brett realized that her words could have a double meaning. One glance at his men's faces confirmed what they were thinking.

'I'll never forget last night,' she continued.

How much longer was she going to toy with him like this? She was staring at him and no doubt she had noted the beads of sweat on his forehead.

'So I'd just like to say thank you, once again.' She surprised him by kissing him in front of all his men. He was so stunned that he was slow to react. Her lips were pressed against his and there was only thing for him to do, which was to put his arms around her and reciprocate and to hell with all the leering faces around him. He was about to take her in his arms when she skipped away from his embrace. She stood a few feet from him with satisfaction written all over her face. She had succeeded in having her revenge. Moreover she knew that he knew that she had succeeded.

10

Several days had passed and Luis and his band of followers were becoming more and more disillusioned. There was no sign of Chianto returning with soldiers from San Caldiz. Moreover the supply of food had run out and on top of that they were having difficulty in getting a regular supply of water. Each time a group of soldiers climbed the mountainside to the stream to fill their canteens the waiting Apaches would take potshots at them. Not that any of the soldiers were killed: the Apaches deliberately aimed just to miss the soldiers.

'They're having a game with you,' said Eagle Eye. 'Sometimes they are like children.'

'Some children,' said one of the soldiers scornfully, showing his blood-ied arm where one of the Apache bullets had gone too close to him.

'You must have moved,' said Eagle Eye.

'Well I'm not going up again to fetch water,' said another soldier. 'What happens when the Apaches stop playing games and attack us in earnest?'

'You won't come back to tell the tale,' retorted Eagle Eye.

The other soldiers voiced their concurrence with their comrade. It didn't take a genius to work out that Luis had a mutiny on his hands.

'We can't stay here without water,' complained Graciano.

'You can't expect my men to run the gauntlet of the Apaches' bullets,' retorted the sergeant.

'What are we going to do?' demanded Luis, who in the past few days had slipped from being the undisputed leader of the band of men to just somebody with a solitary opinion.

'How much longer are we going to give Chianto?' demanded Graciano.

'Perhaps he won't come back with

the soldiers,' said Luis.

'What do you mean?' demanded the other.

'I only met the President once. At his inauguration ceremony. We didn't exactly hit it off,' confessed Luis.

'What happened?' demanded an interested Rodriguez.

'I had too much to drink,' said Luis. 'I was talking to an old friend whom I hadn't seen for years. I was telling him that the President only got where he was with the help of American money and by massacring hundreds of people in San Caldiz, many of them women and children.'

'We know that's true,' said Graciano.

'Unfortunately the President was standing nearby and he heard my remarks. That's why it's likely that he won't bother to send any soldiers out here to help us.'

'Now he tells us,' said one of the soldiers in a voice loud enough to be heard by the majority of his companions.

'Well, we've given Chianto a chance.

If the President had agreed to send some troops they would have been here by now,' said the sergeant. 'The question is, what are we going to do next?' he echoed Luis's question.

'There's only one thing to do,' said Rodriguez. The group hung on his next words. 'Somebody will have to go to the railway.'

'What's the point of that?' demanded Graciano. 'The railway doesn't go anywhere. It isn't finished yet. The rate it's going it won't be finished this year.'

'Someone should go there to talk to the man in charge — what's his name?'

'Brett Calhoun,' supplied Luis.

'He'll know what's going on in Topez,' continued Rodriguez. 'Alphonso has been there for nearly a week now. There must be some people planning to get rid of him. We've got to find out who they are and what their plans are.'

'Yes, that's a good idea,' said Luis, giving it his seal of approval. 'The sergeant here will send one of his soldiers to meet this Brett Calhoun.'

'There's one other thing,' said Rodriguez.

'What's that?' demanded Luis impatiently. Now that an idea had been forthcoming which involved some kind of action he wanted to get on with it.

'If you send one of us he'll probably be killed,' stated Rodriguez calmly.

'How do you work that out?' asked Luis.

'When this Brett Calhoun arrives with his gang of workers every morning I'll bet my bottom dollar that Alphonso sends one of his men with them to make sure that there's no funny business and that none of them rides off to San Caldiz.'

After a few moments' thought Luis conceded the point. 'What are we going to do then?' he demanded.

'We don't send somebody in uniform, we send somebody in plain clothes. He arrives there early in the morning before the gang have come. He hides in the bushes. When the gang have arrived he slips in among them. To

59

all intents and purpose he is one of them. He works with him during the day and finds out what he can about any plans to take over Topez,' said Rodriguez.

'Yes, that seems a sound plan,' concurred Luis.

'The only question is which soldier should we send?'

'It's your idea,' said the sergeant. 'You can go.'

The rest of the soldiers didn't try to hide the smirks on their faces. Rodriguez had been a troublemaker with his suggestions about doing things this way, or that way, ever since he joined the platoon. At the thought that he would now have to work as hard as the railway gang some of the men grinned openly.

11

There had in fact been some movement towards forming a committee to try to restore the rightful rulers of Topez. The committee had adopted the grand title of the Committee of the Revolution. If their title seemed to be an exaggeration, their number did not portray any confidence in their ability to carry out their self-appointed task, since to date there were only four of them.

There was the one who had been unanimously adopted as their leader — the deputy bank manager named Sylvano Cortez. Then there was Fernando Canseco, Eduardo Tomos and Manuel Vastero, who held no particular position of authority but had been happy with the easygoing regime with Luis as mayor and saw no future for them under Alphonso's dictatorship. Of the three, Eduardo presented a dashing figure and boasted of considerable success with the ladies. Although whether his claims were true or not was open to doubt.

'We've got to form a plan,' said Sylvano, at their inaugural meeting.

'The main thing will be to try to release the soldiers from the barracks,' said Eduardo.

'I don't see how we can do that,' said Sylvano, doubtfully.

'It's too well guarded,' opined Manuel, who had joined the committee because his wife, Rosita, had insisted on it.

'There's an old tunnel leading from Pedro's cantina to the barracks,' suggested Fernando. He had joined the committee because he saw it as a way of escape from his wife, Perdita. She was widely recognized as the most nagging wife in Topez and for Fernando to get away from her for even an hour was bliss.

'I didn't know that,' said Sylvano. The other two echoed his surprise.

'I used to work in Pedro's cantina,' stated Fernando. 'That's how I know.'

'And can the tunnel be used?' asked Eduardo, the excitement in his voice matching that on his face.

'Of course,' said Fernando. 'I used to take wine in to the officers that way. They found it was a good way of getting their wine without their wives knowing.' There was a hint of sadness in his voice at the thought that he no longer helped anyone to deceive their wives.

'That's it then.' Eduardo stood up, no longer able to contain his excitement. 'That's our way in.'

'We'll have to take one step at a time,' said Sylvano. 'First of all we must make sure that Pedro is on our side.'

'Let's go to his cantina now,' suggested Eduardo, eagerly.

'We'll discuss it first,' said Sylvano. 'We don't want to rush into this. What do we know about this Pedro?'

'He's my brother-in-law,' said Fernando. 'That's how I used to work in his cantina.'

'Well, will he agree to us using his passage?' demanded Eduardo, impatiently.

'I don't see why not. He hates Alphonso and his gang of killers. Not only that but Alphonso cost him hundreds of dollars when he announced that there was to be free wine a few days ago.'

'Right, this is what I suggest,' said Sylvano, rubbing his hands together. 'It will be up to you to get Pedro's permission to use the passage. You can do it by tomorrow?'

'Yes,' nodded Fernando.

'The next stage will be to recruit more men. We can't do anything with just four of us, even if we can sneak into the barracks.'

'I don't agree,' said Manuel, who had been so silent that the others had almost forgotten he was present.

'Why don't you agree?' demanded Sylvano.

'We're only four, but if we can use the passage we'll have surprise on our side. Fernando can draw a map which will show us exactly where we will come out when we get into the barracks. If we can get to the soldiers and release them we will have a dozen fighting men on our side. Alphonso probably has only about half a dozen men in the barracks. The soldiers should be able to over-power them.'

Later, when he went home to Rosita, he told her about his speech.

'I didn't think you had it in you,' she said, as she cuddled up to him.

'Nor me either,' confessed Manuel.

12

Brett had spent several days trying to get Carmen out of his mind. He would drive his men to work harder, which led to muttered unrest, and during the past couple of days to louder agitation bordering on mutiny. He had not been totally unaware of the men's reaction, but he did not slacken his efforts to drive the men harder.

'You are a hard taskmaster *señor*,' said the bandit, named Philippe, whom Alphonso had designated to accompany the railway workers every day.

'It's good for their souls,' said Brett, enigmatically.

'It's not their souls I'd be worrying about but their bodies,' replied Philippe. 'The way you are driving them, many of them won't be fit enough to carry on laying the railway lines.'

Even Alphonso voiced his disapproval

of Brett's methods. He was called to Alphonso's office one evening after he had finished work. Brett entered the office warily, remembering the last time he had come there, which had been followed by a night in the cells.

To Brett's surprise, however, Alphonso greeted him with a smile and waved him to an empty chair. Brett sat down, regarding Alphonso suspiciously.

'It's all right, *señor*,' said Alphonso, disarmingly. 'I have not brought you here as a result of a complaint. In fact, just the opposite. I hear from Philippe that you have shown every sign of co-operating with my regime — even to the extent of working your men too hard.'

'I've got a job to do. I'm doing it. It's got nothing to do with your regime,' stated Brett.

Alphonso frowned. 'I see you are a man who believes in speaking his mind,' he said.

'The truth has never done much harm. It's the lies and deceit that twist the world into knots.'

'Ah, a philosopher as well,' said Alphonso, choosing a cigar from a packet. He offered one to Brett, who declined. 'Your increased work would have nothing to do with a certain widow of the town, I suppose,' he demanded as he applied a match to the cigar.

'What do you mean?' demanded Brett, hotly.

'It hasn't escaped my notice that after she brought you the tortillas you and she had a public scene.'

'It's nothing to do with you,' snapped Brett.

'Everything that happens in this town is to do with me,' retorted Alphonso. 'How do you think I took over the town in the first place?'

'I don't know. I've never thought about it.'

'I took over the town because one of my spies informed me that Luis and his hunting party would be away at the time. So it was easy for me to bring my soldiers in and take over.'

'Your bandits you mean,' retorted Brett.

Alphonso scowled. 'Don't go too far, señor, nobody is indispensable. Not even you.'

'And I thought I was doing a good job,' replied Brett.

'Up to a point you are, but I require complete co-operation from everyone in the town.'

'All I'm interested in is building a railway. When it is finished I intend going back to the USA.'

'How long do you think it's going to take you to finish it?'

'It depends.'

'On what?'

'On the terrain. On my workforce. And whether I can get my rails and sleepers in from San Caldiz.'

'That's the other thing I wanted to see you about. When do you need them?'

'In a few days' time. I'll be running out by the end of the week.'

Alphonso leaned back in his chair and regarded him thoughtfully. 'How do you usually order your materials?'

'By telegraph, of course, but since you've cut the line I can't do it that way.'

'The line will be restored in the next couple of days. But the telegraph office has been taken over by my men. It will be completely under my control. You will be able to order your rails and sleepers then.'

'In the meantime, I suppose, life goes on as before,' said Brett, bitterly.

'As you say, señor, life goes on. Why don't you just go with the tide? Just accept things as they are. Find a young girl — there are plenty in Topez — the women outnumber the men by two to one. Have some fun. Forget about the beautiful widow. Have a good night out — then maybe you won't push your men so hard in the morning.'

Brett left Alphonso's office. Although he hated Alphonso, his advice stayed with him as he walked slowly back to

The Ritz. How could he forget Carmen when the last time he had seen her had been a few days before? She had obviously been to her husband's funeral and she was being driven past in a coach. He had seen her face through the window. It was not the face of the woman who had taunted him in front of his men. This face was tear-stained: she had obviously been crying. She stared at him as the carriage passed. He could have sworn there was a look of mute appeal as she gazed at him. As the carriage passed she turned so that she could look at him. How the hell could he forget her, he demanded, angrily?

13

Rodriguez joined Brett's workforce without any difficulty. He rode out to the end of the railway at the first light of dawn. He reached the wagons that contained the last consignment of track and sleepers Brett had received from San Caldiz. He hid in the nearby bushes. When the workforce arrived he slipped out from his hiding place while Alphonso's soldier, who had accompanied Brett, was busy lighting a cigar. He joined the workforce to several enquiring and puzzled glances. He put his finger to his lips to ensure their silence. He picked up a shovel without Brett's reacting to the fact that he had inherited an extra workman.

It was when they were having their mid morning break and the guard was some distance away enjoying his tortillas that Brett approached Rodriguez.

'Who are you and what the hell are you doing here?' he demanded.

'My name is Rodriguez. I'm one of Luis's soldiers. At the moment I am dying from digging and carrying rails.'

Brett smiled. 'You'll feel even worse by the end of the day.'

'I can't keep going until the end of the day,' cried Rodriguez. 'If I do I will surely die.'

'You will surely die if the guard realizes that you are one of Luis's men,' said Brett, drily.

'You've got to help me. Luis sent me to find out whether there are any plans to restore Topez back to its rightful government.'

'I wouldn't know. Nobody tells me anything,' answered Brett.

'Somebody must know something,' pleaded Rodriguez.

'I'm just here to build a railway,' said Brett. 'The problems of Topez are nothing to do with me.'

'I see.' The disappointment showed on Rodriguez's face.

'The only thing I can suggest is that you come back into Topez with us this evening. The guard doesn't bother to count the numbers any more. He did in the beginning, but not now. You can find out for yourself what plan there is to take Topez back. Then you can come out with us in the morning and slip away to tell Luis.'

'Thanks,' Rodriguez's heartfelt gratitude was tempered with horror when he suddenly realized that he would have to work all day. 'But how am I going to survive a day's work?'

'I'll give you an easy job to do. I want to know the exact number of sleepers I've got left so that I can calculate how many more sleepers I'll want to order from San Caldiz.'

'Thanks,' said Rodriguez, once more displaying his gratitude.

'Don't be too gushing,' warned Brett, 'or the guard might start to wonder about our relationship.'

Rodriguez finished off the day's work without too many problems. He gave the final figures to Brett. 'There are two hundred and sixty eight sleepers left,' he informed him.

'Thanks,' said Brett.

Rodriguez returned in the wagon with some of the workers who were dying to question him about Luis's intentions. But a shake of the head at the beginning of the journey told them that he had nothing to impart at present. However the very presence of one of Luis's men lifted the spirits of the dozen or so workers. As one of the workers, named Chico, confided to his wife when he returned home:

'Luis must have a plan, or why did he send Rodriguez to join us today?'

'Rodriguez worked on the railway? I always thought he considered himself too clever to do any manual work.'

'Mr Calhoun gave him an easy job after he talked with him. He gave him the task of counting the railway sleepers.

'Mr Calhoun talked with him?'

'Yes, they must have been talking for five minutes.'

'If Mr Calhoun was talking with him, then maybe there is a chance that Alphonso might be thrown out after all. If anyone can help us then Mr Calhoun can. You know that he almost killed one of Alphonso's men with his bare hands when he attacked Carmen.'

'So I heard. I expect Carmen deserved it. She was always flaunting herself.'

'Yes, well she has something to flaunt,' said his wife, with more than a hint of envy in her voice.

Brett's thoughts, too, were centred on Carmen, but as a result of an unexpected invitation. It came in the form of a note which had been slipped under his door while he was away. The note was in large, almost childish, handwriting. It said:

I will be having a wake for my husband. It was his wish. I would like you to come along. Carmen.

He read the note several times, paced the floor several more times, cursed Carmen for the invitation a few times and knew that nothing on earth would prevent him from attending the wake.

14

Fernando was sitting in Pedro's cantina. He was waiting impatiently to have a quiet word with his brother-in-law. Unfortunately, the cantina was full and there was no possibility of Fernando talking to Pedro for some time.

Fernando was drinking a glass of tequila to help pass the time. The only consolation was that the time he was spending in the cantina meant that he was spending less time at home where his nagging wife would be sure to find something or other to complain about.

He thought about their plan to use the secret passage into the army barracks. On the face of it, it seemed a good plan. The passage came out in a cellar in the barracks. The entrance had been carefully concealed under a pile of empty sacks. They should be able to creep into the cellar without disturbing the sleeping bandits. Then it would be a matter of finding the cells where their own soldiers had been locked up. Once they released the soldiers it would be up to them to overpower the bandits. Then it should be easy to restore Topez to its easy, relaxed way of life. He ordered another glass of tequila while he contemplated it.

Of course if the four of them pulled off this coup then they would all be heroes. Including him. He couldn't really picture himself as a hero. Although once he became one maybe his life would change. Maybe his wife would stop nagging him so much. Maybe she would even allow him to come out to the cantina more often. The only reason she had let him come out this evening was because he had convinced her that they had a plan to overthrow Alphonso and his men. Of course she had wanted to know about the plan. He had told her that he couldn't divulge it. She had started railing at him and in the end he had given in and told her that the plan entailed using Pedro's secret passage to the barracks.

To his surprise she had considered the plan thoughtfully and then announced that she thought it was a good idea. He had stared at her with astonishment. When he had recovered from the shock he had informed her that it would mean him spending several evenings away from home while they perfected the plan. To his further surprise she didn't even voice an objection to this suggestion.

So now here he was, drinking his third glass of tequila or was it his fourth? He looked benevolently around the cantina. The trouble was there was nobody to share his new-found good fortune. He was not a regular visitor to the cantina and therefore he found that most of the faces were unfamiliar to him. True, he had helped Pedro from time to time, but his assistance had consisted mostly of running errands, such as taking a bottle of tequila to one of the richer residents now and again, or going down the secret passage to the barracks.

A man who had come to sit opposite him asked him if he would join him in a glass of tequila. That was very civil of him. Maybe he would have just one more glass before he cornered Pedro. The people in the cantina were thinning out and he should soon be able to have a word with his brother-in-law. The man opposite was asking him what was his work.

He explained that he helped out in a butcher's shop. He didn't actually help out with killing the sheep, but he took the meat around on a handcart after the butcher had killed a sheep and cut it up. The man did not seem particularly impressed by the work he did, although he bought him another tequila.

He explained that on market days he helped to run the stall in the market when the butcher was away in a cantina. The man still seemed singularly unimpressed. Fernando took a deep breath. Well, *this* would impress him.

'I'm one of a gang who are going to take over the barracks.'

Why did barracks seem such a hard word to say?

This time the man was impressed. He was so impressed that he bought him another tequila. He even asked him how they intended taking over the barracks. Well he certainly wasn't going to tell him that. But he *had* impressed him, there was no doubt about that.

He was saved from having to make any further conversation by the arrival of Pedro. Unnoticed by him the cantina had almost emptied. 'You can come into the back room now,' said Pedro.

He followed his brother-in-law into the back room. It was funny how the furniture all seemed to have developed awkward corners which he bumped into. He had never noticed them before.

'I've come to ask you a favour,' he said.

'You'd better sit down before you fall down,' said Pedro. Privately he thought that his sister would kill Fernando when he arrived home in this state.

15

Brett presented himself at Carmen's front door. He was wearing a suit, a rare event, and carrying a bunch of flowers, an even rarer event.

She opened the door. In the shadow of the passage he could make out that she was wearing a black dress, but he couldn't see her expression clearly.

'I've brought you some flowers.'

'They're beautiful.'

'Beautiful flowers for a beautiful lady.'

'You shouldn't say things like that if you don't mean them.'

'Who says I don't mean them?'

She led the way into the living room where the wake was already obviously in full swing. Brett vaguely recognized some of the guests — a few of them were even his own workmen, although dressed in their suits and smartened up they were hardly recognizable. Carmen introduced him to her parents. Brett noticed that her mother was still a handsome woman, although now obviously approaching old age. 'We've heard a lot about you,' she said. 'I'd like to thank you for saving my daughter from that attacker the other night.'

'I just happened to be at the right place at the right time,' stated Brett.

'And to break that man's arm when you were fighting with him. You must be very strong,' continued Carmen's mother, remorselessly.

'Don't, mother. You're embarrassing Brett,' chided Carmen.

He didn't mind being embarrassed, particularly when Carmen called him Brett. It was the first time she had used his name and somehow it sounded sweeter from her lips than anybody else's.

He had been to wakes before and knew that the general atmosphere was one of celebration rather than mourning over the late departed. The padre came over to him and introduced himself. He was a small man with a twinkle in his eye.

'I believe you are a Catholic,' said the padre.

'I was brought up as a Catholic,' Brett admitted.

'Carmen guessed you were since she saw the cross on the chain round your neck.'

How had she noticed that, wondered Brett. Then he remembered how close their heads had been when he had been in prison. She must have noticed it then.

'Talking of Carmen,' continued the padre, 'may I give you some advice?'

'I'm always open to advice,' stated Brett, blandly.

'I wouldn't like to see her hurt. Oh, I don't mean physically, I mean spiritually.'

With those enigmatic words he excused himself and moved on to another member of his flock. Brett had a few casual words with members of his workforce who saw it as their duty to come across and introduce their wives to him. Although by disposition Brett did not enjoy functions of a social nature, he found that he was quite enjoying the evening. Carmen finally came across to refill his glass.

'I see you've met the padre,' she observed.

'He's been giving me some advice,' said Brett, as he accepted the drink.

'About why you don't come to church?'

'No, it's about you.'

She flushed. 'I don't think this is the time or place to talk about me.'

'When can we talk, Carmen?'

'You want to see me?' she asked, almost shyly.

'Of course I want to see you. You know that, don't you?'

'Yes — yes — I suppose so.' For the first time her composure cracked. Brett thought she appeared almost vulnerable.

'If we were in America I would come

to knock on your front door in the evenings after I'd finished work. I would ask you to walk out with me. You would agree and we would walk through the fields or up the mountain. We would stop now and again to kiss. You would pick some wild flowers, maybe you would put one of them in your hair. It would be a perfect evening.'

'You paint a lovely picture, Brett,' she said, her voice trembling.

'Well?'

'That's in America,' she said, defensively.

'It's only twenty-five miles away. Things can't have changed much in that distance.'

'You don't understand. America is free. There you could do what you liked. Here, we're under Alphonso's heel.'

'Dictators come and go. Alphonso won't last too long. Maybe a few weeks, maybe a few months, but there'll be some plans to dethrone him.'

'When he is, then you can come to call for me.'

Brett was stunned. Until now they had been a couple in perfect harmony. Now she had delivered a body blow.

'You're not serious?'

'I've never been more serious. Alphonso killed my husband. While he is still in charge of this town I will not go out with another man. Even though I love him,' she added the last words so quietly that Brett was almost undecided whether he had heard them.

Somebody else claimed Carmen's attention and Brett suddenly found that he had lost interest in the party. As soon as he could he made his excuses and left. He said goodbye to Carmen's mother, by taking her hand and kissing it.

'Don't stay away too long,' she said, enigmatically.

16

Luis and his men eagerly awaited Rodriguez's return. When he did eventually arrive at their camp he was greeted with a sarcastic cheer.

'Here he is — the one who's been spending all his time in the cantinas in town,' said one soldier.

'Having at least one square meal a day,' said another.

'Being close to women,' said a third.

'Flirting with them,' said another. 'If you've been seeing my wife I'll kill you.'

'If you've been seeing my wife you can have her,' said yet another. There was general laughter.

'All right,' said Luis, 'Let's have your report.'

'Well there's some plan to try to get rid of Alphonso. I met this man in Pedro's cantina. He told me there was a scheme to take over the barracks. He didn't say any more because Pedro appeared on the scene and they went into the back room.'

'He didn't say when this plan would be put into operation?'

'No, if I had asked him any more questions he would have become suspicious.'

'Well at least that's hopeful news,' said Ballisto.

'Pity we don't know how much longer we'll have to wait in this hole,' said the sergeant.

'There is one possibility of getting some other soldiers back into town,' said Rodriguez.

'How can that be done?' demanded Luis.

'Well, according to Brett Calhoun, Alphonso's guard no longer counts the workmen in the morning. That's how I was able to slip into town and come back easily. So we could get one person each day back into Topez. It's not much, but it's a start.'

Several soldiers clamoured for the

chance to be the first to be selected.

'Does it have to be a soldier?' demanded Ballisto. 'My wife will be worried sick, wondering what's happened to me.'

'It's got to be a soldier. And one who's tough,' asserted Rodriguez. He explained how he had been unable to cope with the hard physical work, and that if Brett hadn't given him the task of counting the sleepers, he would never have lasted the day and the guard would surely have spotted him.

'Well, that lets me out,' said the plump soldier, regretfully.

'I guess Diego's the strongest soldier,' said the sergeant.

Diego was a strong man who had once been part of a circus act where he would bend iron bars and pull a cannon towards him.

'Yes, well, Diego can go to start with,' agreed Luis. 'At least it will be one less here to try to give food to.'

'Food,' said the plump soldier. 'What's that? I haven't seen any since we left Topez.' Everybody laughed.

Brett did not bat an eyelid when Diego turned up for work the following day. He found time, however, to talk to him during the morning break.

'Is this going to be a regular procession?' he demanded.

'That's the idea,' said Diego. 'If we can get several of us into the town this way, we'll be ready when the gang try to take it over.'

'So there's going to be an attempt to kick Alphonso out?' asked Brett.

'Yes, that's what Rodriguez found out.'

'I see,' said Brett, thoughtfully. Maybe what had started as a black day wouldn't be so gloomy after all. Brett had assumed, after hearing Carmen's ultimatum the previous night, that he might have to wait weeks, or maybe months before Alphonso would be overthrown, and he would be allowed to call on her. 'When is this *coup* going to take place?'

'Well, Rodriguez wasn't able to find

out exactly when. He was talking to this feller in Pedro's cantina. He said they had a plan to take over the town.'

'Well let's hope it's sooner, rather than later,' said Brett. 'Anyhow you look as though you're coping with the work all right. The last one didn't manage too well.'

'I used to be a strong man in a circus,' said Diego. 'I should be able to manage all right.'

Brett returned to the solitude of his cabin while the men carried on with their work. If, as the strong man claimed, there was going to be a *coup* shortly then his relationship with Carmen should be able to be put on the rails again. He had been staggered the night before last when she had announced at the wake that she wouldn't see him again until Alphonso had been dethroned. The announcement had been so unexpected, especially since he could have sworn they were getting on so well together. And this had been confirmed by her final whispered words, that she loved him. Any euphoria he had felt on hearing those words had been dashed by the knowledge that he might not see her for weeks, or months. But the news he had just received had been encouraging. He only hoped that whoever planned to take over the town would put their plan into action as soon as possible.

17

In fact the gang of four, as they called themselves, intended to put their plan into action that very night. They had held a meeting the night before at which Fernando had announced that his brother-in-law, Pedro, had expressed his willingness to let them use the underground passage from his cellar to the barracks. He omitted to inform them that he had returned home drunk and that his wife had told him that if they failed with this plan then she would personally make whatever remained of his life a living hell.

So they had arranged to meet that night in the cantina at closing time. When Luis had been in charge of the town there had been no such thing as closing time. It had been left entirely to Pedro's discretion. Now, however, under Alphonso, all cantinas had to close at ten o'clock.

The four had arranged to come into the cantina individually so as not to attract attention to themselves. Eduardo was the first to arrive. He couldn't wait to put their plan into action. It seemed foolproof. All they had to do was to go through the tunnel, sneak into the barracks, go into the wing where the soldiers were kept, and release them. After that it would be up to the soldiers. After all, they were professionals and should be able to overpower Alphonso's guards, who would probably be asleep anyhow.

He couldn't wait for their return from the adventure. They would be hailed as heroes. There would be no doubt about that. He, himself, would make the most of his new-found fame. He had always thought that his destiny had been to become a hero. He would absorb the adulation as was his right. Particularly the hero-worship of the women. His rate of success among the fair sex had been slightly disappointing of late. But he would be able to put all that behind him when they realized he was one of the four who had helped to save Topez.

The pity was that he would have to share his fame with the three others. They weren't a very prepossessing trio. There was Fernando, for a start. He was an ineffectual weed who let his wife bully him. He was the last person whom anyone would want to share a rostrum with when it came to having a civic ceremony to celebrate their success. Still, if it wasn't for Fernando they wouldn't have any plan at all, so he supposed he would be entitled to share the limelight with him.

The other member of the trio, the deputy bank manager, Sylvano, was just about as ineffectual as Fernando. He couldn't imagine why he had joined them in the first place. The only reason he could think of was that Sylvano just liked the idea of being on a committee. It probably gave him a feeling of power. He certainly wouldn't have it as far as the women were concerned, not with his plain face and protruding teeth. In fact he looked like a buck rabbit. He smiled at the thought.

And what about Manuel? Well he was a bit of an enigma. He never said much, but when he did utter a few words they always made sense. It had been his idea to keep the number of the gang to four. He had argued that that would be enough to creep into the barracks and release the prisoners. It certainly seemed to make sense. If there were a large number of men going through the tunnel they would probably make more noise. Therefore their chances of discovery would be greater.

The other three came in almost at the same time. Eduardo wondered whether it was a bad omen.

'Has anybody got a pistol?' he demanded.

To his surprise it was Sylvano who produced a weapon. The only disadvantage was that it was an ancient, single-shot pistol, more useful for duelling in the past than attacking an armed barracks in the present.

'Is that all we've got?' demanded Eduardo.

'It's better than nothing,' said Sylvano, defensively. 'Anyhow we expect there'll only be one guard on duty. Just the sight of the pistol should persuade him to give up his keys so that we can release the soldiers.'

'I've brought a weapon,' said Fernando. He produced a butcher's cleaver.

The others looked at it askance. Eduardo voiced their reaction. 'We don't expect to chop the guard up,' he said.

'You never know, it could come in handy,' said Fernando, defensively.

After a pause Eduardo demanded. 'Are we all ready?'

They chorused their readiness. Fernando led the way down into the cellar. He held his lamp aloft to show the others the stone stairs. 'They say this passage goes back centuries,' he whispered.

The steps safely negotiated they came to the cellar where there was already a lamp hanging from a hook in the ceiling. Fernando pointed to a low door in the corner.

'That leads to the passage,' he explained. 'Usually Pedro has boxes and empty barrels covering it, but he's moved them for us tonight.'

He approached the door and slid back the bolt. It was covered with rust but moved back surprisingly easily. 'I went this way a few months back. When Luis was in charge,' he explained. 'Watch your heads,' he added.

The journey along the passage was uneventful. They moved slowly with Fernando leading, followed by Eduardo, then Sylvano and finally Manuel.

'This is the tricky part,' whispered Fernando. 'If they've found the door and closed the bolt we won't be able to get out.'

'Let's hope they haven't found it,' said Manuel.

They were on tenterhooks as Fernando approached the door. He lifted the latch carefully. It squeaked slightly, but the noise was no more than a disturbed mouse would have made. Fernando pushed open the door.

They were in the barrack's cellar. They had performed the first part of the operation successfully. All they had to do now was to climb the wooden steps in front of them, go along the corridor and at the end of it they would turn a corner which would lead them to the soldiers' cells.

Everything went as planned. They came out of the cellar on to the corridor. Fernando had put his lamp out, having made sure that they were all safely out of the cellar. The corridor was lit by a lamp which hung from the ceiling about halfway along. This suited their purpose perfectly. It meant that any guard coming along the corridor for whatever reason would not be able to see them clearly. He would then assume that they belonged to the barracks too. The element of surprise would be on their side. It should give them a chance to overpower him before he recovered from his astonishment.

They moved silently towards the end of the corridor. They all knew that this was going to be the climax of their adventure. Fernando was relieved that everything had gone to plan so far. He knew that the guard would be in a cell just round the corner. The door would be open, exactly as it had been when Luis was in charge and the cells then held criminals, not soldiers. He wondered whether he should change places with Sylvano. After all, the deputy bank manager had the gun. On the other hand there would probably be no reason for anyone to use the gun. The chances were that the guard was asleep. They should be able to go inside the cell, Sylvano would produce his gun and persuade the guard to hand over the keys. Then all they had to do was to open up the soldiers' cells and release them.

He peered round the corridor cautiously. To his relief the corridor was empty. He signalled to the others that the way was clear. He approached the guard's cell and peered in. A figure in uniform who was dimly lit by a turned-down oil-lamp was slumped in the chair. This was going exactly to plan. He signalled to the others. They joined him in the cell. Their relief was short-lived. Suddenly the cell door clanged ominously shut behind them. The startling sound caused Sylvano to bump against the guard. He was shocked to see his head roll off. It wasn't a head, it was a turnip! The figure was a dummy dressed up to look like a guard. They knew with sickening certainty that everything had gone terribly wrong.

18

A few miles from Luis's camp, and further up in the mountains, the Apaches were holding a council of war.

'I vote we attack the Mexicans now,' said Blue Lightning.

'We've got to discuss it first,' said White Beard, puffing away at the obligatory pipe before handing it on to the next member.

Blue Lightning could not conceal his impatience. 'The Mexicans are ripe for the plucking,' he stormed. 'They have been in their camp for several moons. We have seen to it that they have had very little food and water. They must be weak. We can attack them and overpower them easily. Then we have their prize scalps as well as their rifles.'

'I'm in favour of attacking them and getting their rifles,' said one of the younger braves. 'My Henry rifle is all right up to a point, but it only fires one bullet at a time. I would love to have one of those soldiers' repeating Winchesters.'

A couple of the older braves indicated that they wanted to express their opinion.

'You'll all have your say,' said White Beard. 'After all we're a democracy. In fact we've been a democracy for hundreds of years. The word democracy is one I've learnt from the Pale Faces,' he added, apologetically. 'We used to call it Talking among Equals.'

Why doesn't the old fool get on with the vote? fumed Blue Lightning. They've wasted enough time as it is. He couldn't wait until he had several more scalps hanging from his belt. It would make him in one fell swoop the chief warrior in their pack. He would be entitled to wear the extra feather in his headband. At that moment his neighbour passed him the pipe. He knew that protocol demanded that he should take a deep puff from it. He had often suspected that there was a slight amount of opium mixed with the tobacco, but so far he hadn't been able to prove it, since the mixture was prepared by White Beard's squaw. The opium had the effect of dulling their senses. It gave them a good feeling. It made them think that life was too good as it was to take the risk being killed in a battle. Even though, having being killed, you would merely join your ancestors in the Eternal Fields. The opium stopped them from going out straightaway and attacking the Mexicans. Well, he wasn't going to let it dull his senses. He deliberately took a small puff on the pipe before handing it to his neighbour.

Another member of the council was now holding centre stage.

'I'll be glad when we get back to our own country,' he was saying. 'I'd prefer being chased by the Texas Rangers to being holed up in this country.'

There was a murmur of agreement from a few of the others who were seated around.

Blue Lightning did not know what to make of it. Did this mean that those who were in favour of returning to America wanted to do so without having first attacked the Mexicans who were down by the prairie? Or did they want to attack the Mexicans in the first place and then return to America with their spoils? He glanced around at those who comprised the council. About half were too old to fight. They would certainly vote for leaving things as they were. The other half were younger braves, but none of them had as many scalps in their belts as he had.

The time for the vote was drawing nearer. White Beard spelled out exactly what they were voting for.

'Those who are in favour of attacking the Mexicans straightaway in a battle in which several of you will undoubtedly be killed will put a white stone into the bag. Those in favour of carrying on as we are and harassing the Mexicans so that they will get weaker and we will eventually be able to overpower them with no loss of life on our part will put a black stone into the bag.'

The old fool has put the decision very cleverly, thought Blue Lightning. By making a straight choice between being killed or staying alive the result would be a foregone conclusion. It was. Fourteen black stones to one white stone.

White Beard announced the decision and it brought a hearty cheer. He also announced that they would smoke another pipe to seal the decision. Well, if Grey Beard thought that he, Blue Lightning, would go along with this decision he could think again. This evening it would be his turn to harass the Mexicans. When they came up the mountain track for their usual supply of water he would be aiming, not merely to make them turn back, but to make sure that they left at least one member of their party dead on the mountainside.

19

The following morning the four who had broken into the barracks had been brought face to face with Alphonso. They had spent the night not only locked up in the cell with their neighbours but mostly locked up with their own thoughts since nobody seemed to want to discuss their predicament with the others.

'What have we here,' said Alphonso, who seemed to be in a jovial mood. They were in his office accompanied by several guards. 'Last night's visitors? You really shouldn't have bothered to call at night. You could have come here in the daytime. I would be prepared to meet you. After all, I'm meeting you now, aren't I?'

The four stared at him dumbly.

'Such silent visitors, too,' continued Alphonso. 'I'll bet you had more to say while you were discussing how to break into the barracks last night. But we'll come to that in a minute. If my arithmetic is correct, and I was never too good at arithmetic, there are four of you here now. So what I want to know is, are there any more of you?'

Again there was silence.

'It's a simple question,' continued Alphonso. 'Are there five of you, or six, or even seven? Who's going to answer?'

Nobody spoke.

'What about you, Sylvano? You worked in the bank. You must be good at figures. How many more of you will be expected to visit us again another night? Cat got your tongue?' This time the mask on Alphonso's face slipped and he shouted out the question. 'How many more are you?'

'None. None,' babbled Sylvano. 'I swear it.'

'I don't think we allow any swearing in my office,' said Alphonso. He nodded to the guard who raised his rifle butt and cracked Sylvano on the side of the

110

face. The guard was about to repeat the treatment when Alphonso shook his head.

Sylvano was now lying on the floor alternately groaning and whimpering. The side of his face was a mass of blood.

'You see what happens to somebody who doesn't answer my questions immediately,' said Alphonso, conversationally. He turned to Fernando. 'How many are you?'

'Four,' Fernando answered with alacrity.

'There, that wasn't too bad, was it? Only it's not the correct answer,' Alphonso snapped.

'Not — not the correct answer,' Fernando stammered.

'I make it at least five,' stated Alphonso, calmly.

Pale-faced and trembling, Fernando was unable to gather his thoughts. He stared at the guard who had taken up a position to give him the same treatment as he had given Sylvano.

'You mean if we include Pedro,' said Eduardo.

'Ah, I see we do have a mathematician among you,' said Alphonso, rubbing his hands. 'There, that was quite easy wasn't it?' He directed his remark to Fernando.

Fernando found his voice. 'Pedro wasn't in on the plot,' he gasped.

'Oh, I agree he isn't one of you four. Otherwise I would have seen him here. Unless, of course he was the invisible man.' Alphonso laughed uproariously at his joke. The others smiled sheepishly, except Sylvano who was lost in his own world of pain and suffering.

'What are you going to do with us?' asked Eduardo.

'What am I going to do with you? Now that is a good question. A very good question. First I've had to ascertain that there are not going to be any more misguided nightly excursions into the barracks. I think I've satisfied myself on that point. Now it's time for me to introduce the person who was responsible for your capture last night. Please step forward, Manuel.'

For the moment the implication of Alphonso's statement didn't sink in. Then the others stared at Manuel with loathing.

'You don't think I could have arranged all this on my own without a spy in your camp? Manuel was my eyes and ears. He did an excellent job. He will be rewarded with his thirty pieces of silver.'

'You bastard,' Eduardo swung round on Manuel and would have hit him but one of the guards restrained him.

'What are we going to do with them?' demanded another guard.

'Take them away and hang them,' said Alphonso, contemptuously.

20

There were four soldiers, which was the usual number, detailed to fetch water from the stream for Luis and his party. They did not view the task with favour since the presence of the Apaches had made their journey more and more dangerous. It was all right for Eagle Eye to claim that the Apaches were like children and that they were really playing with them. But children can sometimes overstep the mark and in this case if that happened somebody could really get hurt.

If they could have seen Blue Lightning, who was waiting for them a thousand or so feet up the mountain it would have strengthened their belief that any resemblance to the Apache and a child was fictitious. Blue Lightning was wearing his full war paint. He presented a truly frightening sight. His face was completely covered in blue and red paint so that only his eyes were visible. He had taken up a position where he knew the soldiers would approach him, along a narrow path where only one could come at a time.

'The sooner we give up this way of life and go back to Topez, the better,' said one of the soldiers.

'If we go back to Topez we'll all end up in prison, like the rest of the platoon,' pointed out his companion.

'Well, I'd rather end up in prison than be shot by the Apaches,' continued the other. 'At least if we were in prison my wife and children would be able to meet me. I'd have a chance to see them. Out here all we can see is the prairie, and these mountains. And I don't feel safe in either place.'

Above them, perched like an eagle on his rock, Blue Lightning watched their approach. He calculated that they had a couple of hundred paces to come before he could pick off the first man. He licked his lips — which had suddenly become dry. There was a horrible taste of the paste he used to put his war paint on. He spat it out impatiently.

★　★　★

'It's all Luis's fault,' opined one of the soldiers.

'How do you say that?' asked the leader.

'If he hadn't led us on that wild-boar hunt, we'd all have stayed in Topez and Alphonso wouldn't have been able to take over the town.'

'Nobody could have known that,' protested the other.

'There was no need to have taken so many of us with him. He could just have taken half a dozen instead of twenty men.'

'Yes, I suppose so,' the other conceded, 'but if you remember we were all happy to go. It was a day out for us. We all enjoyed it — until we learnt that Alphonso had taken over the town while we were away.'

Blue Lightning adjusted his aim slightly. Another hundred paces and the first soldier would be in range. He had complete faith in his ability to kill him at that distance. The Henry rifles were ideal for this purpose. He was surprised that he felt so calm. Of course it would be after the killing that he would feel the excitement. It always was that way. He was about to lick his lips again when he remembered the nasty taste of the war paint, and refrained.

'It's ironic, isn't it?' said the soldier who was bringing up the rear and who hadn't spoken until then.

'What is?' asked the one in front of him.

'Luis set up this boar hunt to drum up some support for himself. There's an election coming up and he thought that if he could bring a wild boar back and everyone could have a fiesta, his popularity would rise. Instead of which Alphonso is in charge of the town and Luis is stuck out here.'

'We didn't even get our boar,' said the leader.

'Well, we did get it, but the Apaches took it from us.'

'And we've been living on rabbit stew ever since.'

'I don't want to see another rabbit as long as I live,' said the leader.

In fact he would never live to see another rabbit. A single shot rang out. He staggered and fell. Blue Lightning patted the muzzle of his rifle affectionately.

21

The day after the four tried to break into the barracks would always be known as Black Tuesday in the annals of Topez. At first, though, it started as a normal kind of day. The usual activities took place in the square. The usual old folk walked their dogs. The usual stall-keepers set up their stalls with their vegetables, or second-hand clothes, or knick-knacks. The usual tortilla stalls were in evidence. Even the old army captain, whom people said was not quite right in the head as a result of the gunfire during the Civil War turned out to polish the old cannon which stood on the corner of the square.

It was about ten o'clock that the people started noticing an odd activity — soldiers were erecting a long pole in front of the barracks. The passersby stared at it inquisitively. It was about fifteen feet long, a few inches in diameter and the triangular poles at each end to support it were dug deep into the ground. Concrete was then poured into the holes to make sure that the structure was rock solid. Soldiers stood on guard to stop any children straying on to the concrete before it was set.

The watchers tried to guess what the long pole was going to be used for. 'Perhaps Alphonso is going on a boar hunt,' suggested one. 'The pole would be ideal to tie the boar to.'

'I can't see Alphonso going on a boar hunt,' replied his neighbour. 'Especially after what happened to Luis when he went on his boar hunt.'

'Perhaps he's going to hang some other animals from it,' suggested another. 'Like rabbits.'

'He wouldn't want a pole as thick as that to hang rabbits from,' came the scornful reply.

'What about flags?' suggested a third.

'It looks like a flagpole.'

'Flagpoles stand up the other way,' came the even more scornful reply. 'And anyhow it wouldn't want to be set in concrete at each end just to hold a few flags.'

'We'll just have to wait and see,' stated another.

Some time later in the afternoon the concrete was set hard enough to use the pole. There were only a few people around since many were still enjoying their siesta. The few who were there saw an unforgettable sight. Four soldiers proceeded to suspend ropes from the pole. The watchers' blood froze as they realised the significance of the act. They held their breath, hoping against hope that they were wrong. Perhaps the poles were even now to be used for some other purpose rather than the one which had sprung to their minds.

Their eyes were glued to the large gate in the barracks wall through which the soldiers had disappeared. The suspense became unbearable. If what their reason told them was correct who were the four who were going to be hanged? Surely not four of them? What crime had any four of the townsfolk committed that deserved a hanging? Their minds avidly seized other possibilities. Perhaps it was four soldiers? Whose soldiers? Luis? But he was miles away from Topez and it did not seem reasonably possible that Alphonso had captured four of Luis's soldiers. They grasped at the last straw. Perhaps Alphonso was hanging four of his own men. Maybe they had committed some crime which warranted such drastic action. They clung to the hope until they saw the four men being carried out by the soldiers. Even though they were gagged and bound they were instantly recognizable as Sylvano, Eduard, Fernando and Pedro, who kept the cantina.

The soldiers carried them to the ropes and proceeded to put their heads through the nooses. They presented a pathetic sight. They struggled in the arms of the soldiers, but others came to the soldiers' aid and in the end there were four heads protruding through four nooses.

Alphonso appeared from the barracks. He came across until he was standing by the four figures.

'This is what happens to anyone who dares to try to take over my town,' he shouted.

By now the group of onlookers had swollen to a considerable size. They shivered with collective fear as the implication of Alphonso's words sank in.

At a command from Alphonso the gags were taken off the four figures who were then hauled into the air so that they were hanging a couple of feet off the ground. Their movement upwards caused the nooses to tighten. Alphonso watched impassively.

Those who witnessed it say that the men's screams were the most terrible sounds they had ever heard, worse even than the sounds of men dying who had been shot in the war. As the four bodies swung freely from the iron bar, the four screamed almost simultaneously. As the ropes cut into their necks they gasped for air. Then after a few moments they screamed again, but now the screams did not rend the afternoon air at the same time.

Their families had been summoned by friends. When they arrived they saw the terrible sight. Some rushed forward with the obvious intention of cutting down their loved ones, but were prevented from reaching them by the line of soldiers who stood with bayonets drawn facing the townsfolk.

Alphonso had remained near the hanging men after his original pronouncement. There was a smile of satisfaction on his face. Some say that the smile became more pronounced at each scream of the hanging men.

The priest appeared. He rushed over to Alphonso. It was obvious that he was pleading desperately for the men to be cut down. But Alphonso stood impassively ignoring his protestations. Finally two soldiers led him away.

It was obvious to the silent assembled crowd that nothing would prevent the four from finally stopping their convulsive movements and giving up the ghost. In turn the four realized the same fact. They had, by now, become very weak. Their screams had almost ceased entirely. But at least a couple of them found the breath to curse Alphonso and wish him eternal damnation.

There was almost a collective sigh of relief when the last body stopped twitching and its lack of movement told the watchers that the four were indeed dead. At that realization a curious thing happened, which also has been recorded in the annals of Topez. As if by an unheard command all those assembled in the square went down on their knees. They prayed silently for the souls of the four departed. Those who were near to Alphonso saw that his smile of satisfaction was replaced by a scowl for the first time that fateful day.

22

It was late when Brett returned to Topez. He had stayed behind after his men had returned into town because he needed to check some figures and distances. He knew that if he were a few inches out in his calculations it could affect the direction the railway should be taking and he would find himself hopelessly off course.

He was finally satisfied that his calculations were correct. He mounted his horse and set off at a steady trot towards Topez. His thoughts turned to Carmen, as they so often did of their own volition when he was alone. The ultimatum she had given him, that there would be no point in his courting her until Alphonso was finally ousted, gnawed at him. Who did she think she was, giving him a condition like that? Alphonso might be in power for weeks, months, or even years. Where did that leave him? True, he had a railway to build, but there would come a time when his thoughts could turn to settling down. Maybe starting a family. To do that one needed a wife. Somebody who would be with him for ever and a day. Not a person who said maybe tomorrow we will get together. He was aware that time was passing. He was thirty-two, which wasn't old in terms of becoming a husband, but it could be considered old in terms of starting courting. Damn it, he wanted to start courting Carmen now, not some vague date in the future.

His thoughts were still on her when he rode into Topez. Darkness was beginning to descend and so at first he did not notice the contraption with the four tell-tale ropes hanging from it. When he did spot it, he pulled his horse up sharply. He dismounted without taking his eyes off it. He knew what it had been used for. It had been used to hang four men.

A familiar figure materialized by his side.

'You're late,' said Carmen.

'Who did they hang?' growled Brett.

'Sylvano, Eduard, Fernando and Pedro who kept the cantina.'

'The bastards,' said Brett, viciously.

'I know. Come home with me. I've got a meal waiting for you.'

The invitation took Brett by surprise. He tied up his horse, and followed her towards her house. The square was deserted where normally there would be several people strolling about in the cool evening air. In fact it was unnaturally quiet. The only sound was the swish of Carmen's skirt as she led the way down the alley towards her house.

He followed her inside the house. There was the delicious smell of a home-made stew.

'Sit down.' She indicated a chair in the living room. 'I'm afraid you'll have to eat on your own. I'll be back when you've finished your meal. If you want more there's plenty in the pot — help yourself.'

So saying she disappeared. There was a washbasin on the sideboard. Brett took advantage of it to wash his hands.

He set about enjoying the meal. She had also provided some freshly baked bread. He didn't know when he had enjoyed a meal more. But the enjoyment was tempered by the knowledge that a terrible tragedy had happened in the square that day.

He had finished and was sitting back in the chair enjoying a cigar when Carmen reappeared. She caught the satisfied look on his face.

'That was lovely, Carmen. It's the best meal I've had for ages.'

Normally there would have been a satisfied smile on her face at the compliment. But there was no response from her as she cleared the dishes away. Brett stubbed his cigar away in the grate and waited for her to join him. When she eventually did so, he asked, 'What did the four do?'

'They broke into the barracks last night. Well three of them did, Pedro let them use his cantina to get into the barracks. That's why he was hanged with them.' She said it in matter-of-fact tones which Brett knew managed to conceal her distress. He wondered whether any of the four had been related to her.

'There was a passageway from Pedro's cantina to the barracks?'

'Yes. Fernando used it regularly to smuggle tequila into the barracks.'

'I didn't know any of the three of them, except Sylvano. I wouldn't have thought they were the best three for taking on Alphonso's men.'

'There were four. Manuel was the fourth. He betrayed them.'

'The bastard. I'm sorry.' He held his hand up apologetically.

'It's all right.' Her face by the flickering fire showed no emotion.

'What happens next?'

'It's up to you.'

'What do you mean?'

'You're the only one who can help us. The men trust you.' Suddenly she seized his hand. 'There must be some way of outsmarting Alphonso.'

They sat like that while the grandfather clock ticked the seconds away. Carmen clung on to his hand as though it were a lifeline which she thought could save her.

'I don't know.'

'You mean you don't know whether you will help, or you don't know if you can help.' She showed that she intended drawing her hand away.

'I don't know if I can help. We'd need a plan.' He covered her hand with his other hand.

'Then you will help?' Excitement leapt to her voice.

'If I can.'

She heaved a huge sigh of relief. 'I know you're a good man,' she said, slowly.

'I'm not that good,' he said, with a half smile. There was no responsive smile from her. 'There's only one way out of this situation,' he informed her.

'What's that?' she demanded, eagerly.

'We've got to bring Luis and his men back into town.'

'How can that be done?'

'He sent one of his men in with my gang yesterday. He's the strong man, Diego. The idea is to bring in one of Luis's men every day. But it will take too long. The only answer is to bring them in all together in a single day.'

'Can you do that?' Her eyes burned brightly by the light of the lamp.

'I think so. Luis's guard doesn't check how many men I take out and bring back. I usually take out thirty-six men every day. I take them out in three wagons.'

'How many soldiers has Luis got out there?'

'Twenty-one, so Diego informs me.'

'But you won't be able to get the extra men into your wagons.'

'Listen, this is how it can be done.' He took a salt-cellar, a pepper-pot, and a sauce-bottle from the sideboard.

'Three wagons, right?'

She nodded to show that she understood.

'I usually take twelve men out in each wagon. On the morning we decide to act I take out five men in each wagon. I'll have to distract the guard while the men are getting in. The wagons are covered and so he won't be able to check them.'

'I can distract him,' she said, eagerly. 'I'm sure I can do that.'

'I don't want to get you involved,' he said, doubtfully.

'I am involved, Brett Calhoun,' she replied, passionately. 'I want to help.'

'All right. I take out five in each wagon. Diego has already informed Luis that twenty-one soldiers will be returning with me. These will be hiding in the hills not far from the end of the railway. I will create a diversion first thing in the morning by using some dynamite which I will have prepared the night before. This will give Luis's soldiers a chance to join the gang. It will also mean that they won't be expected to work a whole day, since it's hard work, and unless they are used to it they won't be able to keep up. In which case the guard could spot them and become suspicious. In the evening they all come back into town. If the guard checks the number he will find that there are thirty-six men.'

'Brett Calhoun, you're a genius.' For the first time that evening there was a smile on her lips.

'What we've got to do is to decide which day Luis's men can come into town. I'll have to inform the other men that they won't be coming out with me that day — at least, only fifteen of them will.'

She seized his hand which lay idly on the table. To his embarrassment she lifted it to her lips and kissed it.

'I knew you were a good man,' she said.

23

It was decided that Friday would be the day when Brett was going to bring Luis's soldiers into town. Diego had been dispatched to Luis's camp to explain the situation.

'The day after tomorrow all of us will be going into Topez in Brett Calhoun's wagons,' he informed the assembled group.

'That's good news,' said one of the soldiers, 'Especially with the Apaches picking us off.'

'How does he intend taking you all back into Topez?' demanded Luis.

Diego informed them of Brett's plan. There was a chorus of agreement among the soldiers that it was worth trying. Diego had refrained from informing them about the public hangings of yesterday, but now he broke the news.

At first there was only disbelief, then anger erupted. There were several lurid descriptions of what they would like to do when they got hold of Alphonso.

'There'll be plenty of time for that when you attack the barracks,' said Luis. 'In the meantime clean your guns and check your ammunition.'

'We could do with some oil to clean our guns,' one of the soldiers pointed out.

Diego produced a bottle. 'With the compliments of Brett Calhoun,' he announced, handing it to the soldier.

'He thinks of everything, doesn't he?' observed Luis, enviously.

'Let's hope so,' said the sergeant.

Brett was wondering the same thing as he went about his work. When he had explained the plan to Carmen everything had seemed straightforward. It was true the guard didn't bother to check the number of workers in the wagons. He had become lax during the past couple of weeks. But what if things changed? What if Alphonso had given strict instructions that everything had to be thoroughly checked in the light of the abortive attempt on the barracks? If so the guard would want to count the number of workers going out. He would soon spot a discrepancy between five in a wagon and the expected dozen.

Of course a lot would depend on Carmen. She would be distracting the guard. He had no doubt that she would play her part to perfection. She could play the coquette. At times she could appear to be a superficial person, but he knew that underneath there was a deeply caring one. She cared about her family, her town and, he hoped, about him.

His mind dwelt on the time he had spent in her house the night before last. When he had finished explaining his plan she had stared at him with luminous eyes. Suddenly, without warning, she had come over and sat on his lap. He put his arm around her waist. Their heads were close together. She impatiently brushed a curl away from her forehead. Their lips were close, exactly as they had been in the prison when she had expected him to kiss her. That time he had baulked at the opportunity. But not this time. Their lips met in a long, satisfying kiss.

When they broke apart she regarded him with a half-smile. 'You do know how to kiss,' she stated.

'I used to read about it in books,' he replied, blandly.

'How is it that somebody who read books about kissing isn't married?'

'Maybe I haven't met the right pair of lips.'

'Maybe you'd better check on these again.' She kissed him, more passionately than the first time. At last she said, 'You haven't answered my question.'

He hadn't intended telling her about the way his brother had taken his fiancée from him, but he told her in a flat emotionless voice. When he had finished she kissed him again, this time even more passionately.

'Thanks for telling me,' she said,

huskily, when they finally broke apart.

'Maybe I didn't know how to kiss properly at that time,' he said, with a twisted smile.

'I'm glad,' she said, simply.

She reached across and took a cigar from the packet on the table. She handed it to him. She lit it from the lamp with a spill.

'You know I'm beginning to like this treatment,' he said, as he puffed at the cigar.

She stared at him intently. 'You don't have to go back to your hotel tonight,' she said, slowly.

'You know what you're saying?'

'I'm a big girl now. I know exactly what I'm saying.'

'When we go to bed together I want it be as man and wife.'

'You're a good man, Brett Calhoun,' she said, taking his cigar from him and kissing him.

'So you keep telling me,' he replied.

24

Friday dawned, to all intents and purposes just like any other day. A few sparse clouds flecked the sky, hinting that it was going to be hot later. Brett had been up early. He had gone down to the stables where the horses were kept.

'You're early this morning,' said the stable-owner, through a yawn.

'There's plenty of work to be done,' countered Brett.

'You're driving your men too hard,' retorted the other. 'One of these days you'll find some of them won't be turning up.'

How right you are, thought Brett, as he steered one of the horses between the shafts of the wagon.

Carmen, too, was early. The three empty wagons were waiting in the corner of the square when she appeared. She wore a red-and-black dress with a wide white belt that accentuated her figure. As one of Brett's workmen had said, she had more curves than the Rio Grande. And here she was showing them off for the benefit of the guard when he appeared.

She came over to Brett. He yearned to take her in his arms, but knew that he too must play a part.

'Hullo, Gorgeous,' he said.

'I bet you say that to all the girls,' she replied, with the half smile to which he had become accustomed.

'Only to special ones.'

'What have I got to do to be special?'

'You've got to wear a pretty dress.'

'Does this dress meet with your approval, sir?' she gave a twirl that lifted her skirt above her knees.

'It looks all right from where I'm standing.'

'Perhaps if I came closer to you, you might be able to look at the dress properly.'

She sidled suggestively up to him. Out of the corner of his eye he saw that his men were getting into the wagons. Carmen was playing her part perfectly. Brett knew that he had to respond. Although where they were standing was hidden from the barracks by the high wall, he knew that Alphonso had spies everywhere who could be watching and then reporting back to him.

'Yes, I think the dress suits you.'

She moved closer to him. He pretended to try to grab her. She evaded his grasp and skipped away, laughing.

At that moment the guard appeared. He was leading his horse across the square.

'Now's your chance,' Brett whispered.

They both held their breath at the approach of the guard. When he was near enough, Brett said, 'The men are in the wagons, ready.'

'I'll just have a look,' said the guard.

'Aren't you going to say good morning to me?' demanded Carmen, taking up a provocative stance.

'Certainly,' said the guard. 'Good morning, Carmen.'

'I've just refused the Irishman a kiss, but I'd be willing to give a handsome Mexican a kiss.'

The guard hesitated. He knew that it was his duty to look inside the wagons. In fact he was supposed to count the exact number of workers and then see that the same number returned in the evening. But lately he hadn't bothered to do so. It was obvious to anyone that the same number were going to come back as went out. So he would always glance quickly inside the wagons just to give the impression that he was not shirking his duty. But now another possibility had occurred. It was obvious that the desirable Carmen fancied him. It went without saying that he would give a week's wages — no a month's — to have the opportunity to seduce her. If he managed to seduce her he would be the envy of the garrison. His status would shoot up and he would be regarded as second only to Alphonso himself in importance.

'Well?' Her leg was thrust provocatively forward so that it showed the tight contours of her hips.

Brett mounted his horse. He knew that this was the moment of truth. If the guard refused Carmen's offer then the whole scheme would blow up in their faces.

Carmen emphasized the fact that she was offering her body to the guard by undoing the top button of her dress. The guard didn't need a second invitation. He stepped up to her and took her in his arms. Immediately Brett gave a signal to the drivers of the wagons. They began to drive away. The guard looked up, realizing that he hadn't given the signal, but Carmen's next word held him a prisoner.

'I'll be free, tonight,' she whispered. 'How about one more kiss?'

The guard responded as any red-blooded Mexican would do. The wagons had already disappeared. What the hell? To taste the delights that

Carmen was offering would make up for having to gallop to try to catch them up. He must be the luckiest man alive in Topez this morning.

25

To Brett's relief he and the wagons arrived at the work-place before the guard. He had a momentary pang of jealousy when he thought how many kisses Carmen was bestowing on the guard to keep him occupied. However, he quickly ignored it as he went about the task of getting Luis's men, who had been hiding in the nearby bushes, to join his workforce. He also had to hide their rifles in one of the wagons under some sacks. He managed to complete the operation just in time.

The guard arrived looking flushed. 'You must have hurried to get here so quickly,' he remarked.

'I've got some dynamiting to do,' replied Brett, calmly. 'I want to get on with it, so that the men can get on with their usual work.'

The guard nodded to show that he

accepted the explanation. In fact he would have accepted any explanation that Brett had put forward. This morning he had had ten minutes of pure bliss when he had held Carmen in his arms. This evening there was the promise of more delights to come.

He watched idly as Brett prepared some dynamite and lengths of fuse wire. All the workers were sitting around. Why was it that Carmen was more desirable than any other woman he had ever met? She was beautiful, certainly, all his comrades agreed that she was the most beautiful woman in Topez. But she possessed a quality more than that, something which was hard to define. All men when they saw her immediately thought about going to bed with her. She was the most provocative woman he had ever met, yet not in an obvious way, like some of the women he had met in brothels.

Brett had set the fuses and had warned everyone to keep a safe distance away. Well, he certainly wouldn't be going near the dynamite. In any case he himself would be playing with dynamite tonight — he smiled at the thought.

The dynamite Brett was using was intended to blow up a huge piece of granite which stood directly in the path of the railway. Brett first had to drill underneath the rock in order to fix several sticks of the explosive in position. He had then trailed three fuses away from the rock. When he lit them the men watched expectantly as the tell-tale sparks slowly crept towards the dynamite.

When they reached the rock it seemed for a moment as if the sparks had gone out. Then there was a god-almighty bang. The rock crumbled in front of their eyes. The workers involuntarily cheered. Even the guard smiled at the success of the explosion.

The men set about clearing away the rubble. The guard lit another cigar. He wondered whether he should take Carmen a present this evening. What about some flowers? All women liked flowers. There was a flower-stall in the square, which was open until late in the evening. Yes, when they returned this evening he would definitely buy her some flowers.

He idly watched some of the workers clearing away the pieces of broken rock. As he watched it began to dawn on him that something was wrong. At first he couldn't put his finger on what was bothering him. Then gradually it came to him what was wrong. Some of the men weren't the original workers who would come out in the carts every morning and return in the evening. He would swear to the fact that there were several faces among the workmen that were new to him.

They must have switched some of the workmen, probably for Luis's soldiers. The thought hit him like a thunderbolt. He began to scan their faces eagerly. Yes, there were several faces he couldn't recognize. They thought they had been clever, but not clever enough to deceive Philippe Torrens.

The question was, what was he going to do about it? Well it was obvious that he couldn't do anything until they all returned to Topez that evening. Then he would go straight to Alphonso.

Wait a minute. By the time he reported to Alphonso the soldiers would have been whisked away by Luis's supporters to their homes. There would have been at least a dozen fully trained soldiers in hiding in Topez. That would be the last thing that Alphonso would want.

Was there any other way he could prevent the soldiers from slipping away once they arrived in Topez? Yes, there was one other possibility. Soldiers needed guns to function. Luis's soldiers must have brought guns with them. They must have hidden them in one of the wagons. If he could find out in which wagon they had hidden the guns, he would be in a position to take them over.

That really would be a feather in his cap. If he could present Alphonso with a wagon containing the guns it could even put him in line for promotion. Sergeant Torrens would sound very nice. He would also appreciate the extra pay which would go with the promotion. Not to mention the fact that, as a sergeant, Carmen would be sure to accept his advances.

Suddenly everything in the garden looked rosy. He had the rest of the day to find out where the guns were. Then he would wait until they were almost ready to start off for Topez. He would produce his own gun and would take over the wagon.

The rest of the day proceeded without any apparently untoward events. Philippe wandered off a few times during the day to relieve himself behind a convenient tree as he usually did. On each occasion he walked behind the wagons and studied them carefully. When he had completed his investigation he came to a conclusion. The guns were hidden in the furthest wagon. He had seen the tell-tale signs of the sacks which were covering the guns.

Having found where the guns were hidden he could hardly contain his excitement. He considered drawing his gun, facing the men and telling them he would be driving the wagon with the guns back to Topez. Yes, that was an even better plan than his original one. The advantage was that he would be able to start straightaway. He wouldn't have to wait a couple of hours until Brett announced that it was time to break camp and return to Topez.

He went behind the tree once again to relieve himself. The men were still busy clearing the rocks away. Brett had had to use more dynamite to blast the stubborn remains of the granite away. Philippe approached the wagon which held the guns. Nobody seemed to be taking any notice of him. He had produced his own gun and held it loosely by his side as he walked. He could imagine the surprise on the faces of the men when he jumped inside and drove off.

He reached the back of the wagon and opened the flap. The surprise he had imagined was nothing to the real surprise which was stamped on his face when he saw the sergeant sitting inside holding a gun. His reaction was far too slow. The sergeant had fired and blown a hole in his head before his gun even started to come up.

26

Brett and his men had gathered round Philippe's corpse.

'I had to shoot him,' said the sergeant. 'He was going to take the wagon and ride away. We'd have lost all our guns.'

'Yeah, I can see you had no choice,' said Brett. 'The problem is what are we going to do now?'

'We ride into Topez exactly as if we had finished our day's work,' replied the sergeant. 'As far as Alphonso and his bandits are concerned we're just workers coming home in the evening.'

'What about him?' Brett indicated Philippe with his foot. 'He's supposed to report back to barracks when we all return to Topez in the evening. Alphonso will smell a rat when he doesn't turn up. In fact he'll smell a whole barrelful of them.'

'I hadn't thought of that,' confessed the sergeant.

'Does it make any difference?' asked one of the soldiers. 'Once we're in Topez, we'll go into hiding. When the time comes we'll attack the barracks.'

'I'll have to go to Alphonso and explain that the guard has met with an accident,' said Brett, thoughtfully.

'Some accident when half his head has been blown off,' said somebody.

'There is a way. I'll say his head was blown off by dynamite. I'll say that he went nosing around in one of the wagons to check on our dynamite. He accidentally dropped a spark from his cigar on to a stick and it blew up in his face.'

'Wouldn't the wagon have blown up as well?' asked the sergeant.

'Of course,' replied Brett. 'I'll have to blow up one of the wagons as evidence that I'm telling the truth.'

Brett signalled to a couple of the soldiers to carry Philippe's body into the wagon. He fixed a fuse to a stick of dynamite which he placed underneath. The men stared at the slow moving spark. The expected loud bang was followed by the wagon slowly crumbling on to its buckled wheels.

A couple of hours later two wagons rolled into Topez. Brett was riding his horse and Philippe's body was tied to his own horse which Brett was drawing after him. The wagons stopped at their usual places. The men tumbled out.

The soldiers had concealed their rifles and ammunition in the sacks and moved quickly off the square to the houses where they would be concealed. Brett made his way across the square to the gate leading into the barracks.

The guard at the gate stared at him suspiciously.

'I want to see Alphonso,' Brett informed him.

The gate was opened and Brett led Philippe's horse into the compound. He was leading him towards the main door of the barracks when Alphonso himself appeared.

'What have we got here?' he demanded.

'It's Philippe,' stated Brett, blandly. 'He's dead.'

'I can see that,' said Alphonso sharply. 'The question is, how did he die?'

'He was blown up by dynamite.' Brett stared Alphonso straight in the eye.

Alphonso walked around the horse to which Philippe was tied.

'I've been using dynamite today,' explained Brett. 'I'd left one stick in the wagon. Philippe went round as usual to inspect the wagons. He was smoking a cigar. The ash from his cigar must have dropped on to the dynamite. There was a loud bang. What's left of the wagon is still by the railway.'

'It was a stupid thing to do to drop hot ash on to a stick of dynamite,' said Alphonso, coldly.

'He probably didn't realize I'd left one stick behind,' stated Brett.

'Well he's paid for his mistake, there's no doubt about that,' replied Alphonso.

'I'll arrange for you to have a different guard tomorrow.'

Brett walked away, trying to conceal his jubilation. He had fooled Alphonso. He had brought a couple of dozen soldiers into the town who were now hidden waiting for the word of command to attack the barracks. He couldn't wait to share his exciting news with Carmen.

She opened the door at his knock. Her face split into a smile on seeing him.

'The prodigal has returned,' he said.

'If I remember my Bible correctly the prodigal son went away for years. You've only been gone for twenty-four hours,' she replied, as she led the way into the living room.

'An hour away from you seems like a year,' he replied, as he took her in his arms and kissed her.

When they came up for air, Brett said, 'I've got some news for you.' He tried to convey the remark in a flat voice, but his tone betrayed his excitement.

'Alphonso's died of a heart attack,' she said, lightly.

'Well, he might be under attack soon. I've managed to bring twenty-one of Luis's men into town.'

'So the plan worked?'

'Yes, thanks to you. If you hadn't distracted the guard we probably wouldn't have been able to get away with it.'

'I'm glad I was able to help. What happened to the guard, by the way?'

'The sergeant had to shoot him. He was becoming too inquisitive.'

'I suppose he had to go. He seemed quite nice though.'

Carmen went into the kitchen where she finished making a meal while Brett had a wash in the living room. He thought what a perfect domestic scene they presented. As far as he was concerned this scene could be replayed night after night when he returned from work.

Carmen had prepared a meal of roast chicken, potatoes and cabbage. Afterwards she brought in a milk pudding.

'That was perfect,' said Brett.

'I'm glad you approve,' she said, as she cleared the dishes away.

'I also approve of the cook,' Brett said, as he grabbed her around the waist.

She obediently sat on his lap. They kissed as though they would never break apart. At last, when they did so, Carmen said huskily, 'That invitation I made last night still stands, if you want to change your mind.'

'I'm thinking about it,' said Brett.

At that moment there was a knock at the door. Carmen went to open it. She gave a startled gasp as two soldiers forced their way into the house. Brett's reaction was to rise from his chair. The sight of the guns in the soldiers' hands prompted him not to make a further move.

'Alphonso wants to see you.' One of the soldiers addressed the remark to Brett. 'He said you might as well come along too.' He nodded to Carmen.

'What does he want?' demanded Brett, sounding more confident than he felt.

'He just wants to clear a little matter up.'

Carmen was staring at the soldier as though hypnotized. She had gone quite pale. 'What little matter?' she demanded.

'He would like to know how it is that a guard who died by being blown up with dynamite comes to have a bullet in his head.'

27

A few miles outside Topez in Luis's camp the fact that the soldiers had gone off early in the morning had been observed with interest by the watching Indians. They stayed hidden for a couple of hours in case the soldiers returned. When there was no sign of them coming back they hurried noiselessly back to their camp.

Blue Lightning reported the fact to White Beard.

'The soldiers have gone,' he said, excitedly. 'There are only a dozen or so old men left.'

'How do we know the soldiers will not return?' asked White Beard.

'We don't know for sure. But here's our chance to attack the camp.'

'Perhaps the soldiers have gone into Topez,' suggested Small Owl.

'Why should they do that?' demanded White Beard.

'Perhaps they want to take Topez back so that it will become their city again.'

'Yes, that's possible,' murmured White Beard, thoughtfully. 'You say there are only a dozen old men left?' He turned to Blue Lightning.

'That's right. And some of them aren't armed. The soldiers took their guns with them.'

'It's a long time since we attacked any palefaces,' said White Beard, thoughtfully.

'It was over the border in America,' Small Owl reminded him.

'If we attack the Mexicans and kill them all, we'll be hunted down,' said White Beard.

'What does that matter?' said Blue Lightning, impatiently. 'We can go back over the border to our own country.'

The braves looked expectantly at White Beard.

'Put on your war paint,' he instructed them. 'We will attack the Mexicans when the sun is at its highest. The

Mexicans always go to sleep at that time. We should be able to attack them easily then.'

Fifteen braves started to put on their war paint. Blue Lightning, remembering its bitter taste, tried to avoid putting it too near his lips. When they finished they sat around in a circle watching the sun until it climbed to its highest point.

At last White Beard spoke. 'You will soon be going into battle. Remember our glorious battles in the past, even though they were fought north of the border. Remember that we were feared by all of the palefaces. Remember, too, Geronimo. Remember all the injustices we have suffered down the years. Remember how our people have been herded into camps like cattle. Remember how once we used to be a proud nation, but now are forced to live as outcasts from our own country. Remember all these things and you will surely return victorious and with fresh scalps tied to your belts.'

He gave a signal and the Apaches

began to ride off. They had small ponies which they had stolen from the Mexicans but which were ideal for the terrain over which they were travelling. Not that they had too far to travel before reaching Luis's camp.

They reached their destination, having tethered their horses some distance from the camp. They crawled silently towards the tents. Blue Lightning led the way as befitted their future leader. He stopped at a convenient observation position.

From his position he could distinguish what appeared to be a solitary guard on duty. The guard was leaning on his rifle. Blue Lightning noted with satisfaction that he was within rifle distance.

He was all for giving the signal immediately. He indicated that he was going to shoot the guard. He took careful aim with his trusty Henry rifle. The excessive heat made the air shimmer slightly. It shouldn't affect his aim, though. He was lying flat out on the ground in the position he had seen some of the American soldiers had adopted when they were fighting. He squeezed the trigger steadily, being careful not to snatch at it.

The sound of the shot shattered the silence of the afternoon. The guard spun round as the bullet hit him. He stumbled and fell. To Blue Lightning's chagrin he realized that he hadn't killed the guard, but had merely wounded him. Still, they didn't have time for him to try a second shot. He signalled to the other braves who began to ride towards the tents, uttering their blood-curdling cries as they went.

The Mexicans began to poke their heads out of their tents. They were met with a flurry of lethal arrows. Some of the Mexicans had revolvers and fired at the braves who were now circling the tents. The guard who had been shot joined in the battle and managed to topple one of the braves. Luis, who had joined the fight, was shooting at the braves as they circled the tents.

For a few moments it looked as

though the Mexicans were holding out. There were several dead or dying Indians on the ground, testifying to the superiority of their revolvers over the Indians' arrows. But when Blue Lightning and his men changed their tactics and began to fire burning arrows into the tents, the course of the battle changed too.

The Mexicans, who had been shooting from the comparative safety of the tents, were now forced to flee to try to reach another source of cover. Unfortunately there was none. They became easy victims of the Apaches' arrows. Luis himself was struck by an arrow in the chest. As he fell he realized that he would never be mayor of Topez again.

The victorious Apaches returned to their camp with their prized scalps and also with the guns they had removed from the corpses of the Mexicans. For a while the Apaches celebrated, just as they used to in the past.

28

Brett and Carmen were facing Alphonso in his office. Raw anger was stamped on the bandit's face.

'I'm waiting for an explanation,' he snarled.

Brett came up with the only explanation he could think of. 'He was shot. By an Apache. They attacked us. The guard managed to drive them off, but as the last one rode off he was shot by an Apache brave.'

'You expect me to believe that?' Alphonso thumped the desk with his fist. Brett shrugged.

'It's true. Ask any of the men.'

'That's what I intend to do, first thing in the morning. After I've hanged you.'

'What crime have I committed?' demanded Brett.

'You concealed the truth from me,' growled Alphonso.

'Only because I knew you wouldn't believe it,' retorted Brett. 'Your guard was a hero. He must have killed four or five Apaches before they rode away.'

Carmen was regarding Brett with admiration. She was amazed at the story he had concocted in such a short time. She was even more amazed at the way he was standing up to Alphonso.

'Of course there could be another explanation,' said Alphonso, silkily.

'What's that?' demanded Brett.

'That you are lying through your teeth. That either you or one of your men shot Philippe.'

'Why would we want to do that?' demanded Brett.

'I haven't got the answer to that yet,' confessed Alphonso. 'But you can rest assured that when I do your life won't be worth an American dime. Take them to the cells.' He directed the remark at two of the guards who were standing with rifles poised. 'I will find out the truth in the morning,' he shouted, as they were led out through the door.

Brett and Carmen were locked in adjoining cells. The cells were separated by bars. Carmen approached them and put her hand on them. Brett did the same, touching her hand.

'If Alphonso hangs you, I want to die with you,' she said, simply.

'I hope it won't have to come to that,' said Brett, trying to sound reassuring, but only partly succeeding.

There was a guard on duty who was seated on a stool a few feet away from the cells. Alphonso obviously wasn't taking any chances. Brett racked his brain for some way of getting out of the cell, but he couldn't come up with anything.

Carmen was still holding his hand. She had put her head close to his. 'I love you,' she whispered. 'I wanted to have your children.' She began to weep.

'Don't cry, Carmen,' said Brett, desperately. 'I'll think of a way out of this.'

The minutes dragged by and Brett hadn't come up with a single idea to help them get out of their present predicament. He had searched in his pockets for anything which he might be able to use as an implement or weapon, but he had found nothing. Only a box of matches which he had used to light the fuses on the dynamite. He surveyed the matches gloomily when a glimmer of an idea occurred to him. He examined it. It seemed far-fetched, but it did offer a faint possibility of escape.

He whispered his plan of action to Carmen.

'It sounds too dangerous,' she whispered warningly.

'It can't be more dangerous than being hung in the morning,' he replied.

'Be careful,' she said, warningly. She kissed his hand before releasing it. Brett checked that the guard was still on his stool. Satisfied, he then lit a match and applied it to his mattress. At first there was no smell of smoke. Brett wondered if the mattress was too damp to burn. He was about to light a second match when a thin spiral of smoke rose from the mattress.

Brett knew that his next move would have to be timed to perfection. If he acted too soon then the whole plan would certainly fail. He must wait until the mattress really caught fire before alerting the guard.

There was now a small cloud of smoke emanating from the mattress. It was beginning to smell with the pungent odour of burning straw. Brett prayed that the guard wouldn't notice it for a couple of minutes. The longer the mattress burned and the more smoke it created, the better would be his chance of putting the second part of his plan into action.

However the guard did not completely fall in with Brett's plan. He jumped off his stool and appeared outside Brett's cell.

'Your mattress is on fire,' he cried.

'I had some matches in my pocket. They must have started the fire,' said Brett, appearing to be panic-stricken.

He hoped that the guard was too confused to realise how stupid the statement was.

'I'll get a bucket of water,' the guard gasped.

'There's no time. I'll have choked to death by then,' cried Brett, emphasizing the point by going into a paroxysm of coughing.

'I'll open your door. But no funny business,' said the guard, covering Brett with his revolver.

While the guard was fumbling awkwardly with the key in his left hand, Brett had taken off his jacket and was apparently trying to put out the flames with it. In fact he had succeeded in setting his jacket on fire. The guard finally managed to open the cell door. As he stepped inside two things happened almost simultaneously. The first was that Brett flung his jacket which was now burning brightly at him. The guard involuntarily raised his arm to prevent the flame from reaching his face. As he did so Brett hit him with a haymaker which ensured that he would take no further interest in the cell or its fire for some time.

It took only a few moments for Brett to relieve the guard of his keys and release Carmen.

'Come on,' she said, 'let's get out.' She started to move towards the tunnel.

'You go ahead,' he said. 'There's something I've got to do.'

'Let's get out while we can,' she cried.

'I've got to release the soldiers,' said Brett.

He suited the action to his words by going along to the nearest cell and opening it. Two soldiers stepped warily outside. He moved along to the next cell while Carmen waited impatiently at the end of the corridor. The guard in Brett's cell showed signs of recovering. Carmen grabbed the nearest soldier and pointed out the danger. The soldier hit him with all the force that the pent-up tension being a prisoner for several days could bring. For the second time in a few minutes the guard collapsed on to the floor and took no further interest in the proceedings.

Brett had finally succeeded in releasing all the soldiers. Carmen led the way to the tunnel which led to Pedro's cantina. They eventually all came out, dishevelled and dusty but deliriously happy.

'I can't wait to get home to the wife and family,' said one of the soldiers, with heartfelt relief.

'There's something to be done first,' Brett informed them.

The assembled men stared back at him with surprise. Brett explained exactly what he had implied. As Brett outlined his plan the surprise changed to excitement.

★　★　★

Alphonso found out about the escaped prisoners before dawn. He flew into a terrible rage. He had the unfortunate guard who had let the prisoners escape brought to him. Without giving the guard a chance to explain what had taken place, Alphonso shot him.

After a couple of soldiers had removed the body from his office he calmed down. He indicated that he wished to be left alone with Lieutenant Ramires. The latter waited for his chief to speak.

'So now we've got a dozen soldiers ready to attack us when the time is ripe,' he said, as though speaking to himself.

'We can take them easily,' said Ramires, confidently.

'But what if there are more?' demanded Alphonso.

'How can there be more, we only had a dozen in the cells,' said a puzzled Ramires.

'What if Calhoun managed to smuggle the rest of Luis's soldiers into the town. There were at least two dozen out there. If he managed to bring them in, then they would have as many soldiers as we have. In fact a few more, since I've already killed one of ours.' He laughed briefly.

Ramires smiled dutifully. 'How do you think Calhoun managed to bring the rest of the soldiers into Topez?'

'I don't know. I haven't got a crystal ball. But I'd bet that was why Philippe was killed, to allow him to bring the soldiers into the town. I never did swallow that cock-and-bull story about the Apaches having killed him.'

'What are we going to do?' A worried expression had appeared on Ramires' face.

'We'll have to assume that Calhoun and his men will attack at dawn. I want every soldier at his post to defend the barracks.'

Alphonso's guess that Brett and the soldiers would attack at dawn was correct. But he did not foresee exactly how Brett would attack the barracks.

Brett and his men waited until the first grey flecks of dawn had changed into enough light for them to fully recognize their enemy.

'You all know what you have to do,' Brett informed the assembled company. All of them were now on horseback, the horses having been loaned from stables and farmers who had lent them willingly in the belief that it would help the town to get rid of the hated tyrant, Alphonso.

'When I give the signal you ride like bats out of hell towards the barracks,' stated Brett.

'When we get inside we move as quickly as we can to the main building,' added the sergeant. 'After all, we lived inside there for a long time and we know the building like the backs of our hands.'

'That's right,' said Brett. 'Now all we've got to do is wait until we can see them clearly.'

While they were waiting he thought about the tearful farewell he had bidden Carmen an hour or so before. She had pleaded with him not to go. She had pointed out that it was not his fight, he was an American. She had told him that he had done more than enough by bringing the soldiers into town and then releasing the prisoners from the barracks. Her pleading had moved him, but had not succeeded in making him change his mind.

'I've got a job to finish,' he had told her.

She had clung to him. He had finally managed gently to disengage himself. She watched him as he climbed on to his horse.

'I'll be back,' he told her.

Now the dawn had given them sufficient light to make the attack. They were about a hundred yards from the main gate.

'Here I go,' he informed the soldiers. He lit the fuse on a stick of dynamite. He knew that if he had miscalculated or if one of Alphonso's gunmen managed to hit him with a stray bullet he would end up being blown to pieces.

He waited until he was sure that the fuse was lit. He took a deep breath then began to ride like hell towards the barracks gate. Whether it was surprise at seeing a solitary horseman, or for whatever reason, he was not met by the expected hail of bullets. In fact he had almost reached the main gate when a solitary bullet winged past him.

He reached the gate and tossed the stick of dynamite towards it. He couldn't see exactly where it had settled because he was now riding like the wind out of range before it blew the gate and himself to kingdom come.

He had ridden about a couple of hundred yards and was wondering whether the dynamite was going to explode when his doubts were answered by a huge bang. He pulled up and swung the horse around.

The gate and part of the wall had been blown away. There was enough room for an army to go through, he thought gleefully, as he rode back. Many of Luis's soldiers had already entered the barracks compound, having taken advantage of the dust and smoke the explosion had created.

There was hand to hand fighting and the sounds of pistol fire. Brett ignored them as he rode through the compound towards the front door. As he had been riding back towards the barracks he had lit another stick of dynamite. This time he tossed it near to the large oak door and rode away from the prospective explosion. He went round a corner and dismounted.

A couple of seconds later there came the expected bang. Brett rushed towards where the door had been but where now only a crazy gap marked its place. He rushed through the smoke and dust, ignoring Alphonso's men who had been inside the building near the door and were now either lying prostrate on the ground, or wandering around in a daze.

Brett dived down the corridor which led to Alphonso's room. He burst in. Alphonso was busy filling a satchel with notes from a safe.

'You won't need those where you are going,' said Brett.

181

Alphonso involuntarily dropped the satchel. Almost in the same movement he produced a knife from his belt. Brett smiled. Although it appeared that Alphonso held the upper hand, Brett knew otherwise. He had been brought up in a rough Irish district where bar-room brawls were bread and butter to him.

Alphonso paled when he saw Brett's smile. Surely he held the upper hand. He had the knife. He still had time to kill the American and make his escape in the confusion. He lunged for Brett's chest.

For a big man Brett moved quickly. He side-stepped the knife. It tore his shirt but did not come into contact with the expected flesh. When Brett seized Alphonso's arm in a vicelike grip, the dictator knew he had lost. The knife slipped irretrievably from his fingers. Alphonso tried to kick Brett but without success. He screamed as Brett began to apply pressure on his arm. He suddenly remembered how Brett had broken the arm of one of his men. Surely he wasn't going to suffer the same agonizing fate?

He was. A couple of Luis's soldiers came into the room. They stopped in their tracks when they saw Brett was dealing with Alphonso. Brett forced his arm upwards until it could go no further. The soldiers watched with pleasurable anticipation as they waited for the inevitable 'crack'. When it came they gave a cheer.

The battle for the barracks was soon over. Once word was passed out that Alphonso had been captured, the rest of his men who were still alive rushed to their horses and tried to make their escape. Some of them were shot by Luis's men but a handful managed to escape.

'They won't bother us again,' said the sergeant.

Brett rode back to Carmen's house. She was waiting by the door. Her eyes searched anxiously for any signs of injury. She spotted his torn shirt with alarm.

'It's all right,' he said, as he jumped down from his horse. 'It's only the shirt that's damaged.'

'What about Alphonso?'

'He's in one of the prison cells. I expect there'll be a public hanging that everybody will go to.'

'What about us?' she demanded, moving close to him.

'First we'll get married. Then we'll see about those babies you were talking about,' he replied.

THE END

Other titles in the
Linford Western Library:

MIDNIGHT LYNCHING

Terry Murphy

When Ruby Malone's husband is lynched by a sheriff's posse, Wells Fargo investigator Asa Harker goes after the beautiful widow expecting her to lead him to the vast sum of money stolen from his company. But Ruby has gone on the outlaw trail with the handsome, young Ben Whitman. Worse still, Harker finds he must deal with a crooked sheriff. Without help, it looks as if he will not only fail to recover the stolen money but also lose his life into the bargain.